He put two fingers under her chin and tilted up her face. He bent his head and kissed her lightly on the cheek. "Ah no, do not scold me, it was not so very distasteful, was it?"

She put a hand to her cheek. "No," she whispered. "I did not find it distasteful in the least."

He kissed her again, on the lips this time. She made no resistance but put up her hand and stroked his hair, and his arms went around her.

She had not the least notion how this man had managed to awaken in her heart the love she had been seeking in a succession of admirers. She knew now what her mother had meant when she spoke of truly loving a man. She knew that if he did not return her love, then life would be desolate indeed. . . .

Also by the author:*

THE SPANISH DOLL
PRELUDE TO LOVE
THE GENEROUS VINE
VALLEY OF NIGHTINGALES

# TOMORROW COMES THE SUN

## ELIZABETH RENIER

ACE BOOKS

A Division of Charter Communications Inc.
1120 Avenue of the Americas
New York, N. Y. 10036

An ACE STAR Book
by arrangement with
Hurst & Blackett Ltd.

Printed in the U.S.A.

# 1

In the small enclosed world beyond the drawing-room windows nothing had changed. Several fishing smacks rode at anchor close to the New Quay, their crews drinking ale and exchanging gossip on the bench outside the inn. Placidly beneath the evening sun the river flowed down to join the sea beyond the great mass of Dartmouth Castle. On the opposite bank, smoke drifted up through the trees from cottages perched upon the steep slopes. Off Bayard's Cove a three-masted schooner swung to the outgoing tide; a cartel ship awaiting her cargo of French prisoners who had been fortunate enough, by virtue of age or wounds or some influence with the British Transport Office, to gain their repatriation in exchange for Englishmen captured by Napoleon's forces.

It was with a sense of surprise, hurt even, that Crissa Conway remarked the tranquillity of the scene. She would have welcomed, as more fitting accompaniment to the words her father had just spoken, a roll of thunder or a sudden rain squall. At least the sky should have darkened, the sun have been blotted out.

For the brightness in her own world had just been obliterated. No more balls or soirées or pleasant gossip amongst friends. No boating or picnics or delightful walks by the riverside with her choice of a dozen admirers. No secret rendezvous with Harry in the twilight, which made her feel so deliciously wicked. Not for months. And all because Hetty, and not she herself, had been so indiscreet; so wicked, in their father's eyes.

He said, in the clipped cold tone which irked his elder daughter, "I repeat, Clarissa, that you and Hetty will be sent at once to your Aunt Clara at Tavistock."

Crissa stepped forward, hands outstretched in appeal. "Oh, no, Papa. Please do not send us there. It is so . . ." she faltered, seeing from her father's expression that all protest would be fruitless.

He stood before the marble fireplace, tall, erect, his pale face with the hollow cheeks and high-bridged nose framed by the severe legal wig. His black suit appeared too big for his thin frame. There was not one touch of colour anywhere about him. Even his eyes were darker than usual, his lips more bloodless.

Not for the first time, Crissa wished her father was a different type of man. She would rather have endured explosive rage, for she could have matched that with her own fiery spirit, than this icy calmness. Against such self-control she felt herself helpless, and could only clench her hands and strive to control her own anger.

"May I enquire what alternative you would propose, miss?" he asked sarcastically. "Let me put the case before you as I see it. Four months ago I set out for London upon business connected with the most important of my clients, business which took me a great deal longer than anticipated and necessitated my travelling on to Oxford. I set out, I repeat, leaving your sister Hetty in your care. It is not to be thought that I did not have misgivings, since you have always shown a regrettable tendency to inherit the more irresponsible side of your mother's character. However, as you had reached the age of twenty-one and appeared to have abandoned some of your more hoydenish ways, and as you have usually shown a commendable affection and protective attitude towards your younger sister, I trusted you to see that she came to no harm. And what do I find?"

Impatiently Crissa twitched the skirt of her green gown. Her thoughts went off at a tangent as she remembered what Harry had said.

"You should always wear green, Crissa. It matches the flecks in your eyes and makes you look like the autumn woods, all green and gold." Harry spoke so differently now from the teasing manner of their childhood days when he had, to her fury, called her "conker-head."

"Are you listening to me, Clarrisa?" Her father's voice jerked her back to the present. "I repeat, what do I find? Your sister, at the age of eighteen, within three months of bearing a—a bastard."

"That is not true, Papa!" She stamped her foot in emphasis. "Hetty is married. You have seen the proof of it."

"A marriage of necessity," he said with distaste.

"It was not like that at all. Lieutenant Stanhope asked you formally for Hetty's hand at Christmas. If you had let her marry him then, or even become betrothed, this would never have happened."

She saw by his pinched nostrils how angry she had made him. But still he did not raise his voice.

"Hold your tongue, miss. Am I to be dictated to as to whom my daughters should marry? You are perfectly well aware that I have already chosen suitable husbands for you both."

"And thereby assured us years of misery," she retaliated. Then, realising that for Hetty's sake she must curb her tongue, she changed her attitude. "Papa, will you not listen to me, please? I realise this news must have given you a dreadful shock. But nothing can alter what has happened. Hetty fell in love, so deeply that nothing else mattered to her. She was foolish. But she was not wicked. For that foolishness she is paying now most dearly. She is, as you pointed out, only eighteen, and already a widow. Lieutenant Stanhope died honourably when his ship was sunk by a French privateer. That news I had to break to Hetty, barely two weeks ago, and I thought her heart would break." She moved close to him, her hands clasped tightly together. "Lay as much blame upon me as you will, Papa. Punish me as harshly as you deem fit. But I pray you, have pity on Hetty. Forgive her, Papa. Please forgive her."

His expression did not alter. His dark eyes held only contempt. "I bade you hold your tongue, miss. You are too like your mother in looks and voice. You show the same deplorable impulsiveness. You are headstrong and wilful, whereas Hetty . . ." He broke off and struck his clenched fist into his palm. "That *she* could have done this to me," he said with great bitterness. "She has always been so tractable, so ready to listen to reason; so quiet and dutiful."

And so obviously his favourite. Even the way he

8

addressed his daughters was proof of that. To the elder he used always the formal "Clarissa"; whereas it was difficult to remember that the younger had been christened Henrietta. Not that Crissa had ever minded the preference. Her father's nature was beyond her understanding. She had little affection for him and was impatient of the way he brought his legal mind to bear upon every small decision or problem. For herself, she was happy to follow her "deplorable impulses" wherever they might lead her.

But, studying him now from beneath her long lashes, she was suddenly and surprisingly sorry for him. For the first time she saw this unfortunate affair quite clearly with his eyes. His favourite daughter, so like him in appearance with her dark hair and brown eyes, having the same pale, fragile look, had flouted him in the most astonishing manner by marrying secretly a penniless young naval officer who had got her with child. In Thomas Conway's view the marriage was a disgrace; the child due in November all but a bastard. And as a widow burdened with such a child, what chance would Hetty have of a suitable match? That was how he would regard the affair. Though her heart ached for Hetty, Crissa could not help feeling a certain amount of pity for her father.

She said gently, "Papa, I am truly sorry. I do realise what a great blow this is for you. But Hetty..."

"Do not let me hear you speak her name again," he interrupted. "I have already made clear to you, Clarissa, that I utterly refuse to allow her into my presence. I will not be forced to view with my own eyes the evidence of her appalling deception.

You will inform her of my decision. I shall write immediately to your Aunt Clara and send her a sum sufficient to cover all your needs for the next four months. You will be ready to leave the day after tomorrow, which will allow time for the horses to be rested and any necessary repairs to the carriage after my extended journey."

Recognising that she was beaten, that further argument or pleas were useless, Crissa stood before him, auburn head bowed. "May I ask a question, sir?"

"Well, what is it?" he snapped.

"What reason am I to give my friends for our sudden departure?"

"You will have neither the need nor the opportunity to offer any explanation. You and your sister will remain in this house until you set out for Tavistock. You will have no communication with anyone save the servants. I shall inform those whom I think necessary that Henrietta, never strong, has been taken suddenly ill and is recommended a prolonged stay in the more bracing air of Dartmoor, and that you are naturally accompanying her."

She caught her breath. She saw again what this was doing to him, how he would be forced to lie, a heinous crime in his eyes. She made one last effort.

"Papa, Hetty *is* married. It is not really a disgrace that she is with child. And people will have to know, sooner or later."

"Why, pray?"

She stared blankly, not understanding.

"I repeat," he said bitingly. "Why will people have to know?"

"Naturally they will. When we return with the baby, how can it be kept secret then?"

He crossed to the window and drummed his long fingers upon the sill. He spoke very slowly and deliberately.

"I think you still do not understand me. When you return I shall have arranged for Henrietta's marriage. Naturally, the young man of excellent family whom I previously had in mind is now out of the question. But rest assured that I shall find someone who will do well enough. As to this—this child . . ." As he turned and she was faced with those relentless eyes, Crissa knew exactly the feelings of a prisoner against whom Thomas Conway was stating his case.

"As to the child," he repeated in a tone all the more chilling for its quietness, "it is my earnest prayer that it may be stillborn. If it *should* survive, your aunt will know what to do."

"You mean . . . ?" Crissa's voice was little more than a hoarse whisper.

"My meaning should be clear enough. The child will be placed with a suitable family, at some distance from both Dartmouth and Tavistock. When you return home you will behave as if your sister had recovered from a long illness. Not one word about a child or this disgraceful marriage will pass your lips or hers. Is that plain enough?"

She could not answer. She could only stand and gape at him, lips parted, eyes wide with horror.

He strode across the room and caught her wrist in a painful grip. "Do you understand, Clarissa? Or have you lost your wits as well as any sense of propriety?"

11

She tried not to flinch, to meet his eyes without shrinking. In that moment she knew with painful clarity that he was wishing it was she herself and not Hetty who had brought this misfortune upon him. Just for that moment she shared his wish.

But it could not be so. There was nothing she could do, either for him or for Hetty, it seemed. His pride was shattered beyond bearing and his one thought at present was to avenge himself upon Hetty.

She bowed her head. "I understand, sir," she said quietly. "It shall be as you say."

Dismissed, she went slowly upstairs, feeling a further resentment against her father because he had lain upon her the onus of breaking the news to Hetty. It was she, though her whole being rebelled against such a task, who must tell her younger sister that she was to be banished to Dartmoor, placed under the jurisdiction of their formidable aunt, and that her baby was to be taken from her. Crissa paused on the landing, gripping the banister. Her mind recoiled from repeating that last, most cruel injunction and she resolved that Hetty would not learn from her, not yet at any rate, the further heartbreak which was to be laid upon her. When the time came would be soon enough. Perhaps, as her father had said, the child would not live. Then the problem would solve itself. Hetty was young. Should her baby die, as so many did, she would overcome her grief in time, as in time her heartbreak at Peter's death would lessen. But to know her baby was alive, cared for by people she had never seen, perhaps to pass her own child in a street one day and never know. To be forced to banish its existence from her mind as if it had never been conceived. Hetty would never be able to bear that. Nor, Crissa knew only too well, would she.

Her sister was pacing restlessly about her bedroom. She turned expectantly as Crissa entered. Although her pregnancy was scarcely noticeable, Crissa saw with a pang that Hetty had put on her loosest gown and was holding herself in, in preparation for meeting her father.

She shook her head sadly. "It is no good. He will not see you. I am come to give you his orders." Crissa took her sister's cold hand in hers. "Sit down, dearest, while I tell you. And try to be brave."

When the news was broken, Hetty cried out in despair. "Papa will not even acknowledge my baby? Oh, it is not fair. He is treating me as if I were no better than a common trollop off the streets." She rose and walked jerkily towards the door. "I will go and tell him so. He has always shown a certain affection for me. He *can* be kind despite his strictness. He . . ." She broke off as she saw her sister's expression. "You think it would be useless?"

"I am sure of it. You must understand, dear, that it is because he has affection for you that he takes this attitude. You have shocked him dreadfully and upset all his plans for you. Had it been myself he could have borne it more easily. But *you* have never given him a moment's anxiety. *Your* conduct has never caused him any disquiet—until now."

Hetty sank on to the bed and buried her face in her hands. "And he has banished me to Grimstone House with nobody to talk to but Aunt Clara; with nobody by me when my baby is born. How can I bear that?"

Crissa put an arm round the younger girl's shoulders. "I shall be with you, dearest. Did I not make that plain?

Hetty raised a tear-stained face. "You are to come with me?"

Crissa nodded. "And Phoebe to look after us. Perhaps it will not be so very bad, after all."

Hetty clung to her. "I think if you had not been going I could not have borne it, not even for the baby's sake. That is all I live for now, Crissa; Peter's child. When I heard Peter was dead I wanted to die too. I thought of ways of ending my life. Then the baby moved within me and I knew that I must go on living."

Crissa turned away to hide the despair which she feared must show in her face. When she could control her voice she said briskly, "Come now, we must call Phoebe and decide what clothes we are to take. One thing is certain, I fear. They must needs be of the warmest."

For had not their mother described Grimstone as the coldest, dampest house she had ever entered? Was it not likely to be so, set on the edge of the wild and lonely moor which was so often swept by violent rainstorms, blanketed with mist, hidden beneath snow? The house, their mother had complained, was as gaunt and cheerless as its mistress. There was nothing to do there. No company, no music, no gaiety of any kind. The very name of their aunt's house brought back threats and warnings from childhood.

"If you two do not behave, you'll be sent to Grimstone. And you'll not like that in the least, that's very certain."

Now the threat was being carried out. Because Hetty had fallen in love, deeply, passionately, but unwisely. And Crissa had not seen in time what was happening, so engrossed had she been in her own affairs of the heart. But hers had gone no further than a holding of hands in the moonlight and a few innocent kisses, despite all the dire prophecies the gossips had made about her. It had been Hetty, quiet reserved Hetty, who had plunged headlong into disaster.

Despite the tightly shut windows and the rug tucked round their knees, it was cold in the carriage. The raw dampness of the moor penetrated to their very bones. It seemed hours since they had left Plymouth on the second stage of their journey, yet they had covered only a few miles. The road, bad at any time, had been made worse by three days of rain and the passage of heavy wagons taking stores to the new depot for French prisoners at Princetown.

As the vehicle lurched and swayed Hetty held tightly to Crissa's hand while Phoebe, sitting opposite, peered from side to side searching for familiar landmarks in this most westerly part of Devon which was her birthplace. Not that she could see anything but the sodden turf and bracken, and a few bedraggled sheep seeking shelter beneath the windblown clumps of rough heather.

"Us must be nearing Roborough Rock," she told her mistresses, staring through the streaming window. "Then 'tis an up and down road to Tavistock, and after that I'm flummoxed. Your aunt's house be on the road to Okehampton, so Joshua tells me, and that's a road I've never set foot on. 'Tis proper out in the wild, I'm thinking, and no place for an old lady to live on her own."

"Aunt Clara does not live alone," Crissa corrected her. "She has servants, and of course there must be neighbours and . . ."

She broke off as the maid shook her head vehemently. "I don't reckon so, ma'am, not thereabouts. You don't have neighbours on the moor, only in the towns. My mother tells me there's quite a few folks live up to Princetown now. My cousin's married to a farmer there. Doing well they are, supplying milk and cheese and suchlike to the Frenchies in the prison."

"They should be starved."

Startled by the bitterness in Hetty's voice, Crissa said, "You must not talk like that."

"*You* have not had your husband killed by the French. If you had, you would share my hatred of them and wish every one of them dead." Hetty's nails dug into Crissa's palm even through her glove. "I would kill every Frenchman with my own hands if I could, and laugh to see Napoleon burned alive before my very eyes."

"Hush, dearest, hush. You must not upset yourself so. It is not good for you." It shocked Crissa profoundly to see her sister, usually so quietly reasonable, consumed now with such bitterness and desire for revenge. Phoebe sat silent in her corner, her eyes troubled.

Crissa turned to her. "Since you suggest we are to be cut off from the rest of the world, how do you suppose we shall occupy ourselves?"

The maid's forehead creased in thought. "There'll

16

be the sewing and knitting for the baby. And Miss Hetty's things'll need to be let out again afore long. And other little tasks about the house, doubtless."

"And for entertainment?"

"Crissa, you must be joking," Hetty declared. "Surely you cannot have forgotten that Aunt Clara is near to being a Puritan?"

"I am trying hard to forget what Aunt Clara is like," Crissa answered tartly. "We were very young when we met her. Perhaps we were mistaken and she is not as prim and strict as we believe."

"It is useless to pretend, as you so often do, that things are better than they really are. You know perfectly well that we were not mistaken. Why, I recall clearly that Mama dressed us in our plainest gowns and impressed upon us most strongly that we were to be on our very best behaviour when Papa's sister came to visit us."

Crissa sighed heavily. "You are right, of course. I was but trying to put a more cheerful aspect on our stay with her. I suppose one *can* exist without morning calls and musical evenings and dancing, for a few months. And Harry—I wonder if he will remain true to me while I am away."

Her sister's face was stricken. "Crissa, how selfish I have been, I have thought only of my own distress, my own predicament. I have not spared a single thought for what this means to you; that you are being forced to sacrifice yourself for my sake. Oh, forgive me."

Crissa squeezed her hand. " 'Tis no matter. Doubtless the moorland air will do me a deal of good." She glanced out of the window and shuddered. "That is, if it does not put me in my grave. In any

17

case," she made an effort to sound lighthearted, "Harry was becoming a little difficult. I do not think we should really suit each other. Yet he adopts such a possessive air that other young men are quite put off. There is that very handsome young officer staying with the Poultenays, for instance. Despite the encouragement I have given him—most discreetly, of course—I am assured he thinks I am secretly betrothed to Harry."

She was thankful to see that she had made her sister smile. But Hetty's face was serious again as she asked, "Crissa, do you suppose you will ever fall properly in love? Completely and utterly, I mean, as I did with Peter? So that there is no one else in all the world?" Her voice broke.

Crissa squeezed her hand. " 'Tis no matter. Doubtless the present, I find it most gratifying to be admired and sought after; to know that I may raise a young man's spirits or cast him down merely by a word or look. And falling in love every few months is a wholly delightful experience. And falling out of it is not entirely disagreeable, for I know it will not be long before I lose my heart again." She leaned forward to look through the window. "Why do you suppose we have stopped? It must be quite the hundredth time."

The rain had eased a little, so she let down the window and called up to their coachman, "Joshua, cannot you . . . ?" She broke off abruptly, staring ahead.

Trudging along in the thick oozing mud of the track was a straggling column of men dressed in a variety of garments. Some were in torn shirts and breeches, their feet bare, their hair unkempt. A number wore yellow jackets with the letters "T.O." printed on the back. Some limped, some of the weaker ones were supported by their stronger comrades. A few, better dressed, their bearing more erect, walked a little apart. On either side marched a column of militiamen with fixed bayonets, the bright colours of their uniforms dulled by the saturating rain.

"Who can they be?" Crissa wondered aloud. "Hetty. Come and look."

Her sister joined her at the window while Phoebe craned her neck from the opposite side.

"Oh, Miss Clarissa, I know!" she exclaimed excitedly. "They'll be French prisoners from the hulks in Plymouth going up to the new depot at Princetown. I've heard my cousin tell of it. Oh, what a grand sight to be sure!"

"Grand?" Crissa repeated in astonishment. "You can speak so of such misery, such—degradation?"

Hetty's voice held again an unfamiliar harshness. "You surely are not going to express pity for them? Like Phoebe, I rejoice at such a sight. They are our enemies, at our mercy now. I am glad to see them so, *glad*. If I had Joshua's whip I would lay it about their shoulders as we pass, and laugh in their faces."

Horrified, Crissa stared at her sister. Never had she imagined grief could transform a soft-voiced gentle girl into this stranger with blazing eyes and savage tongue. Would she herself feel the same were she in Hetty's place? Would the loss of a loved one induce in her such hatred, such longing for revenge? When their mother died . . . But that was different, she reminded herself quickly. Mama had died of the influenza, and one could not rail against sickness, which was ordained by God. Peter Stanhope had met a violent death at the hands of his fellow men. And those men had been French.

But despite the sympathy she felt for her sister, she could not share Hetty's triumph at the sight of these formerly proud troops of Napoleon reduced to bedraggled scarecrows and plodding along so wretchedly in the squelching mud. Perhaps even at this moment, somewhere in Europe, Englishmen were in the same plight. Their cousin Nicholas might be amongst them, or any of the young men they knew who had left the sheltered valleys of Devon to save the world from the domination of the self-styled Emperor. Had it been Napoleon himself being marched between the lines of soldiers, then she would have rejoiced as wholeheartedly and been as fierce in her triumph as Hetty. For that upstart Corsican, so she had heard her father declare, was responsible for all the misery of war, and for the threat to England's safety which persisted even in this year of 1812.

"Why does Joshua not drive past?" Hetty demanded peevishly as the carriage trundled heavily forward a few yards, then stopped again.

"He cannot do so," Crissa told her, having a better view. "The road is too narrow."

"Then the Frenchmen should be made to stand aside. If the wheels go over them, so much the better."

Crissa was about to admonish her sister for her uncharitable attitude when she noticed the look of strain on Hetty's face and how pale she was. She reminded herself that Hetty was with child and the feelings of women in that state, so she had been told, were sometimes unnatural.

Phoebe, attempting to humour her young mistress, said brightly, "They'll turn off afore long, I think, Miss Hetty. The road to Princetown goes off to the right, but we go north for Tavistock."

Crissa was about to sit back when she heard the sound of hooves on the road behind them. A horseman, his blue caped coat spattered with mud, his beaver hat darkened by rain, drew alongside the rear wheels of the carriage. Seeing the two girls at the window, he raised his hat perfunctorily.

"Will you have the goodness to instruct your coachman to pull to one side that I may pass?"

"It would be of little use, sir," Crissa answered. "There is a solid mass of men ahead blocking the road. That is why we are held up."

"And that is exactly why I wish to pass," he said tersely. Frowning, he pointed with his whip. "See, another poor fellow has dropped out. He will be prodded on at bayonet point if I am not there to stop it."

"Why should you wish to do so?" Hetty questioned. "If they fall out they must naturally be made to go on."

The man raised dark eyebrows. "Even if they are wounded, and their feet cut and bleeding?"

"They are French," she said, her lips set in a thin line.

"So that makes them not human in your opinion? I am afraid I do not share your view, madam. Furthermore, I am a physician and care not what nationality a sick man may be. I pray you let me pass that I may help that wretch by the roadside."

Crissa, leaning further from the window, was about to call instructions to the coachman when Hetty dragged her back.

"No, do not bid Joshua pull aside for anyone who helps our enemies. Let this man make a detour if he is so anxious to get by."

The horseman, hearing her words, burst out furiously, "If you think I am going to risk breaking my neck amongst those boulders, you are mistaken, madam."

He brought his whip down sharply on his horse's flank. As the animal leaped forward, the rider's spur scraped noisily along the polished panels of the carriage. Mud splashed on to Crissa's cheek. About to make an angry protest, she found the stranger's face on a level with her own, and was immediately silenced. For no man had ever looked at her like that. His dark eyes blazed with scorn. His mouth showed clearly his disdain.

"I am scarce the man to be thwarted by women's callousness," he said. " 'Tis generally supposed that you are the gentler sex. I never knew that idea proved so false as now." He took off his hat, revealing his dark curly hair, and bowed to them in a manner wholly contemptuous. "May God reward you for your charity, in His own way."

"Sir, you do not understand," Crissa began. But he was out of hearing, cantering towards the man lying by the roadside, shouting to the soldier who stood threateningly above the prisoner.

Crissa discovered that she was trembling as she pulled up the window. She saw that Hetty, too, was upset by the incident.

Phoebe exclaimed in an awed voice, "Fancy any

gentleman speaking to you like that, Miss Clarissa!
Proper insolent he was, to be sure."

To her surprise, Crissa heard herself excusing the
stranger. "He had cause, I think. We—we hindered
him in what he considered his duty. Hetty, I wish
you had let me call to Joshua to draw aside."

"Does it matter?" her sister retaliated. "Is it of
any consequence what a country doctor with
French sympathies thinks of you? Must you have
every man's eyes wide with adoration, only admiring words on their tongues?"

Crissa was stung to protest. "*Hetty!* How dare
you speak to me like that?"

Hetty changed in a moment. She buried her face
in her hands and her shoulders shook.

"Oh, Crissa, I am sorry. I do not know what is
happening to me. I am so terribly unhappy and
cold and my body aches so."

Crissa took her sister in her arms, wrapping the
rug more closely about her. She took off Hetty's bonnet and laid the girl's head on her own shoulder,
comforting her as she had done all through their
lives together. She blamed herself for not having
seen that Hetty was at the end of her endurance;
that whatever lay ahead could hold for the younger
girl only grief and pain, and the terrible fear of
the unknown. Whatever her sister said or did under these circumstances must be excused. It was
her own task to bear with her, no matter how difficult that might prove.

Crissa's spirits sank as they continued their journey. The streets of Tavistock were all but deserted
and there were no lights to be seen in the grey
stone houses. For it was August, not November as

the weather suggested. The northerly wind, blowing down off the moor ahead of them, rocked the carriage. Rain beat with renewed force upon the windows. It was cold enough inside the conveyance. For Joshua on the coachman's box, and young Daniel the footman clinging on behind, conditions must have been well-nigh unbearable, Crissa realised.

Gently, so that she would not waken Hetty who had fallen into an exhausted sleep, Crissa eased her aching arm.

"How much further have we to go, do you suppose?" she asked Phoebe.

"Joshua said your aunt's house was little more than a mile or so out of Tavistock. But he's only been the once so far as I know. It's to be hoped he knows where 'tis." She peered through the streaming pane. " 'Twouldn't surprise me if we ended up in a bog, or got benighted. A proper Dartymoor day, this be, as I remember well enough from my childhood."

"You mean we are like to get such weather often?" Crissa asked in dismay.

The maid nodded with gloomy satisfaction. "For sure. The moor's well known for its bad weather. Up to Princetown where they've took the queer notion to build the depot for French prisoners, 'tis worse than anywhere. How any of them survive the winter, the Lord only knows."

Hetty would say it would be all to the good if they did not, Crissa thought. Recalling the effect of her sister's sentiments on the young doctor, she hoped that he was from Plymouth and there would be no likelihood of their encountering him again.

Above the wind she heard Joshua shout to Daniel

to hold on tightly. The carriage swung sharply to the left.

Phoebe peered from the window. " 'Tis no more than a narrow lane we'm on, and proper steep so far as I can see."

After a few minutes of swaying and lurching, they halted and the springs jerked as Daniel jumped down. He trudged through the mud to open an iron gate set between two granite pillars. As the vehicle moved forward again Crissa saw that they were entering a rough drive between stone walls beside which beech trees had been planted to form a wind break.

Phoebe said in a subdued voice, "It don't look a very cheerful place, do it, Miss Clarissa?"

"I did not expect it to be," Crissa answered ruefully. Impulsively she stretched out her hand. "Phoebe, I am very glad you are with us. We shall need your help. At least, poor Hetty will. She is so young to bear all this."

"Don't 'ee worry, ma'am," the maid said stoutly. "I'll take good care of her. Nobody'll be unkind to Miss Henrietta if I can help it, not even your Aunt Clara." She glanced out of the window and drew her cloak more closely around her. "There's few folks as can scare me. 'Tis other things I'm afeard of . . . things not of this world. And there's plenty of that sort in these parts."

"Oh, come, Phoebe," Crissa chided her. "You surely do not believe in ghosts?"

The maid leaned towards her and spoke in a lowered tone. "You don't know the moor, Mis Clarissa. There's things as happen in the wild places as none can't explain. There's Lady Howard's coach, for instance, that's haunted the very road we've just come along, for hundreds of years. 'Tis driven by a headless coachman and my lady sits inside staring straight ahead and her face ashy white. Alongside the coach runs a black hound that has to pluck a blade of grass from Okehampton Castle every night till there be no more left. And there's Dewer and his wish hounds," she went on hurriedly as Crissa was about to interrupt. "He's the devil in disguise, and if you were to meet them at night, alone on the moor . . ."

"I am very unlikely to be alone on the moor, especially at night. Phoebe, I will not listen to such nonsense and you are not to repeat such stories to Hetty."

Gently Crissa roused her sister. "Come, dearest, we have reached the end of our journey at last. Daniel has lowered the steps. Phoebe will help you."

Only half awake, Hetty stumbled down and stood under the stone portico, looking vaguely about her as if she had no idea why she had come to this place. Crissa joined her and waited for the door to be opened in response to Daniel's tug at the bell rope.

There was nothing in her immediate surroundings to raise her spirits in the least. The square-built granite house, its windows tightly shuttered, appeared hemmed in by trees which swayed and creaked under the wind's onslaught. The damp cold lapped around her like a wet blanket. She shivered, pulling her cloak more closely about her. Hetty had forgotten to put on her bonnet and her dark hair, blown loose, whipped across her pale cheeks. The horses hung their heads dejectedly. Joshua stamped up and down, slapping his arms across his chest and grumbling to himself.

"They're a long time coming," Daniel remarked, giving the bell another tug.

"Perhaps Aunt Clara thought we would not travel on such a day," Crissa said. "Had you better go round to the back and . . . ?"

She broke off as she heard a bolt being pulled. A key grated in the lock. The door was opened a fraction. An old woman with a pock-marked nose and small black eyes, her face topped by a huge mob cap, peered round the edge.

"D'you think I'm deaf?" she demanded in a high querulous voice. "Well, what d'you want?"

"Is this not Grimstone House, Miss Conway's residence?" Crissa asked doubtfully.

" 'Course 'tis. Oh, I see, you'm her nieces. Why didn't you say so? Well, come inside. Don't stand there in the rain. And wipe your shoes. And you"— she glared at Daniel. "Don't 'ee go trapesing mud all over the floor when you bring in the boxes."

Phoebe giggled, with the result that the glare was transferred to her. The old woman opened the door only just wide enough for them to enter.

Crissa looked about her. They were in a dim, musty-smelling hall. The walls were covered with faded tapestries and above the staircase hung portraits in heavy frames, interspersed with antlers and foxes' masks and one mangy head she assumed was that of a wolf. Over the marble mantelpiece was an array of axes and swords and pistols, flanked by two shields bearing coats of arms. Dimly in one corner she could make out a suit of armour.

She heard Phoebe's smothered exclamation of dismay. Hetty clutched at her arm.

"It is worse even than we imagined," the younger girl whispered. "It feels as if it is not even lived in."

Hearing footsteps on the stairs, Crissa silenced her sister. A woman appeared on the first landing, a tall thin woman dressed in a black gown which made not the slightest concession to fashion. Even in the half-light Crissa could recognise the resemblance to her father, although his sister's hair, beneath the unbecoming muslin cap, was white and her skin wrinkled. The high-bridged nose which gave him a distinguished air was, in Aunt Clara's case, regrettable. It jutted bonily from her thin face and emphasised the deepset eyes.

"Heaven help me," Crissa thought in dismay as her aunt unhurriedly descended the stairs. "I shall no more be able to avoid those eyes than I can Papa's. No wonder poor Mama was daunted by Aunt Clara."

Dutifully she curtsied low and waited for the elderly woman to greet them. Aunt Clara advanced slowly and with dignity. The servant opened a door to the right and motioned the girls to go inside. Hetty still clung fearfully to Crissa's hand.

"Open the shutters," Aunt Clara ordered. "It is too early yet for candles."

In the poor light which filtered between the trees, their aunt unsmilingly surveyed them both.

"Clarissa," she said coldly, "you are regrettably like your mother in looks and, I am led to believe, in nature. I did not approve of her. It is most unlikely I shall approve of you."

Crissa gasped. She had not expected a warm welcome, but this was so unfair she was tempted to protest. But her aunt had turned to Hetty.

"As for you, Henrietta, I am beyond speech at your conduct. That a member of our family, which has been so highly regarded in this district for generations, could so disgrace . . ."

"There is no disgrace," Crissa broke in hotly. "Hetty is properly married and you are not to . . ." The desperate pressure of her sister's fingers stopped her. "I beg your pardon, ma'am," she said with forced meekness. "The journey has been very cold and tiring. If we might be allowed . . ."

"*Clarissa!*" Her aunt's voice was like her father's, the very quietness of her tone more daunting than if she had shouted. "I think we had better understand each other from the start. This is *my* house and *I* decide what happens here. When I consider it is time for you to be shown to your room, you will go. Until that time, you will kindly keep silent unless I invite you to speak."

Crissa clenched her hand inside her cloak and bit hard on her lower lip. Had it not been for Hetty she would have marched straightway from this forbidding house and ordered Joshua to take her to the nearest inn. As it was, she took a deep breath and said as docile as she could, "Very well, ma'am. As you wish."

"Let this be perfectly clear to you," Aunt Clara went on in the same acid tone. "You are not welcome here, either of you. Only the close ties of our family and loyalty to my brother made me agree to take you in. Nor could the timing and circumstances be more inconvenient. From the very start I shall

lay down certain rules regarding you and my other—guest."

Crissa's head jerked up. Her father had not mentioned that there would be anyone else staying in
the house. Impatiently she waited to learn who it
might be.

The clipped voice continued. "You will not, under
any circumstances . . . Clarissa, are you listening
to me?"

Crissa certainly was not. Instead, she was staring
incredulously at the figure in the doorway. A young
man of slender build and most handsome features
stood hesitantly there. He wore tightly fitting grey
trousers with the fashionably tasselled Hessian boots,
and a brown cut-away coat above a striped waistcoat. His fair hair was cut in the new mode, short
at the back and sides with curls on his forehead.
He had the bluest eyes she had ever seen. His appearance was so astonishing in this house that she
continued to stare at him even after she had heard
her aunt's exclamation of annoyance.

The young man seemed as disconcerted as herself. He came forward uncertainly and bowed to
all three ladies.

"*Pardon*," he said to Aunt Clara. "I fear I intrude.
I had no idea your visitors had arrived."

There was something odd about the way he spoke
though Crissa could not at once decide what it was.

"You wished to speak to me?" Aunt Clara asked
coldly.

The young man spread his hands deprecatingly.
"It is of no consequence now." As his eyes met Crissa's the expression in them was so familiar in its
open admiration that she felt her spirits lift at once.

If this young man lived nearby, life need not appear quite so hopeless.

"These ladies are your nieces?" he asked, and again she was struck by his odd pronunciation.

"They are," Aunt Clara answered grimly. "And although you will have little communication with them, in common courtesy I consider it my duty to introduce you. Clarissa, this is Lieutenant Armand de Beauvoir of the French navy, who is staying in my house as a prisoner on parole."

Crissa caught her breath. As she held out her hand, she dared not even glance at Hetty. The young man raised her fingers to his lips, and bowed again.

"*Enchanté, mademoiselle.* I very much hope that your aunt will not be so cruel as to deny me your company. I should be devastated if . . ."

"And this," Aunt Clara's voice cut sharply into his pleasantries, "is my younger niece, Henrietta, Mrs. . . ." Her nostrils narrowed as she faltered over the name.

"Stanhope," Crissa supplied hurriedly.

The Frenchman turned to Hetty. Her face was drained of colour. She half raised her hand. Then, quickly withdrawing it she turned her back on him. As she made for the door her steps were unsteady. She swayed and caught at a chair back for support. Crissa started forward. But it was Armand de Beauvoir who reached Hetty first and caught her as she fell.

## 2

"Hetty, come and look," Crissa cried delightedly as she opened the window shutters next morning. "The sun is shining and the grass full of spangles. You can see for miles and miles. Why, the moor is almost beautiful."

"You call that beautiful!" Hetty exclaimed incredulously as she joined her. "It is a wilderness, so vast and empty. I am sure there is not a living thing on those bleak highlands."

Crissa laughed. "You do not use your eyes. There are some sheep."

"*Sheep!*" her sister echoed disgustedly, turning away.

Crissa was determined to start the day lightheartedly. "You should not speak so disparagingly. They provide mutton for the table and wool for your back. Look at those strange tumbled rocks on the skyline. They must be what Phoebe calls 'tors.' " She opened a window and leaned out. "How very neglected the garden is. But then, I suppose it is difficult to grow . . . Oh!" Hastily she drew back.

"What is the matter?" Hetty asked.

Crissa pulled the frilled collar of her dressing-gown more closely around her neck and rearranged her curls.

"It is Lieutenant de Beauvoir at work on one of the flower beds. I—I believe he saw me."

In fact she was sure he had done so. She was

also well aware that he was now leaning on his spade, looking towards their window with great interest.

"Crissa, come away," Hetty's tone was shocked. "Do not, I pray you, start your tricks here or you will get into dreadful trouble."

"I have not the slightest notion what you mean by my tricks," Crissa remarked airily. "How was I to know that our fellow guest would be outdoors so early? I surmise he has to work in the garden as a kind of punishment. Though, to be sure, I would have thought to be billeted in this house would be punishment enough."

Hetty dropped on to the hard chair beside the window. "Crissa, how am I to bear it? Was it not enough to be banished here, to be treated as if I had committed an unforgivable sin? Am I not tortured enough by the thought that I shall never see my beloved Peter again, without the knowledge that under the same roof is a man who might well have given the order which—which caused his death?"

Crissa moved to put an arm around Hetty's shoulders, then changed her tactics.

"That is foolish, dear," she said crisply. "Monsieur de Beauvoir was taken prisoner nine months ago. He was here at Grimstone when Peter's ship was in action. Hetty, you must try to overcome this prejudice. You cannot suppose this young man wishes to be here any more than we do. Phoebe tells me there are well over a hundred French officers in Tavistock alone."

"It should not be allowed. They should have been shot as soon as they were captured."

Crissa sighed impatiently. "Suppose your Peter had been taken prisoner, or cousin Nicholas, or any other young man we know who is fighting for his country? Would you have the French shoot *them* out of hand? You cannot have one-sided rules in war, Hetty."

Her sister looked stubborn. She shuddered with an exaggerated action. "I cannot bear the thought that he even touched me."

"You are being absurd. Monsieur de Beauvoir behaved with the utmost chivalry yesterday. Nobody could have lifted you more gently or carried you upstairs with greater care. If you would have preferred Daniel to aid you, you should have come out of your faint and said so. There, now I have upset you. I am sorry, Hetty. But you must not constantly entertain these bitter thoughts. I know how deeply you grieve for Peter, but you must not, for his child's sake as well as your own, allow yourself to become so disturbed. We are here to stay by Papa's orders, and Monsieur de Beauvoir is here by Aunt Clara's invitation. We cannot alter these circumstances. We can only endure them as best we may."

"I did not fully understand how it came about that he is here," Hetty said in a subdued voice.

"His grandmother was a childhood friend of Aunt Clara's. She married a Frenchman and has lived in France ever since but corresponded regularly with Aunt Clara. Monsieur de Beauvoir is apparently very like her, which accounts for his fairness and blue eyes which made me think at first he was English and merely speaking in a strange fashion. When Aunt Clara heard he was a prisoner of war she asked that he should be sent here for the length of his parole, and the Transport Board agreed."

"How did you learn all this?"

"From Aunt Clara herself. She explained it all to me most carefully." Crissa giggled. "Perhaps she thought if she did not do so, I should have grave doubts about the propriety of the situation—an unmarried lady harbouring under her roof a dashing young foreigner, and he quite unrelated to her."

"Crissa, you are incorrigible," Hetty exclaimed, joining in her sister's laughter. Suddenly she caught Crissa's hand and laid it against her cheek. "Help me, Crissa dear. Help me to be brave. I am so very frightened."

"There is nothing to fear," Crissa assured her stoutly, and hoped she might be forgiven for the lie. "Phoebe and I will be with you all the time. You do not have to encounter Monsieur de Beauvoir if you do not wish. It certainly seems to be Aunt Clara's plan that we do not meet him. She explained explicitly that he occupies rooms at the back of the house, and that was why she had put us both in this front room and Phoebe in the little dressing room so that there was no need for us to communicate with him in any way."

"By the manner in which he looked at you from the doorway yesterday," Hetty remarked, "I am not at all surprised. I dare say Papa gave you a dreadful reputation in his letter, even though it was I who . . ."

She broke off as there was a knock on the door and Phoebe entered.

"Miss Clarissa, you are to dress at once and go

down to your aunt. She wishes to give you what she terms your 'orders for the day.' "

"I declare it is worse than being in the charge of a governess," Crissa complained. "For though I won many a battle with them, I fear Aunt Clara will beat me every time. She has, after all, the whip hand." She caught sight of Hetty's puzzled expression, but forbore to explain that it was on her sister's account that she was determined not to provoke their aunt. She promised herself the satisfaction, when their stay came to an end, of giving vent to all the frustration and irritation she knew with certainty would be her lot during the coming months. In the meantime, hard though it should prove, she would keep her temper and curb her tongue.

The resolution lasted exactly twenty minutes.

"You are very late, Clarissa," Aunt Clara greeted her niece when she entered the dining room. "I have already breakfasted. You may help yourself from the sideboard. Martha has other things to do than to wait at table twice for one meal."

"I'm sorry, ma'am. I did not realise you rose so early. I will remember in future."

"Where is Henrietta?"

"She begged to be excused this morning. She is somewhat indisposed. I think the journey upset her."

"You will inform her that I expect her to be ready by ten o'clock to accompany us to Tavistock."

"If I may be allowed to say so, I think the jolting of a carriage is not at all comfortable for her."

"I do not suppose it is. But you are mistaken in supposing we shall go to Tavistock in a carriage. It is my custom, when the weather permits, to walk there and back."

"It seemed a considerable distance yesterday," Crissa ventured.

"It is just about a mile to the town."

"I do not think Hetty could manage that, ma'am."

"Nonsense! It will benefit her. Now get on with your breakfast, miss. The routine of this house cannot be disrupted to suit the convenience of when *you* choose to eat."

Crissa helped herself to a slice of cold ham. She was about to take another when she felt her aunt's eyes on her and hastily put back the cover on the silver dish. When she sat at the table, Aunt Clara stood opposite her, tall, black-gowned and forbidding.

"Clarissa, I have been questioning your maid regarding your clothes. It appears they are most unsuitable."

Crissa laid down her knife and fork. "Aunt Clara, you seem to forget that I am twenty-one and therefore quite old enough to choose my clothes with some degree of good taste. I assure you, they are quite *à la mode*."

Her aunt's face was expressionless. She did not raise her voice. Crissa experienced the familiar helplessness which beset her whenever she attempted to reason with her father.

"I am not concerned as to whether they conform to what is, in my opinion, a deplorable fashion. I am merely informing you that thin petticoats and even thinner gowns may be sufficient for you in Dartmouth. You will certainly not find them so here.

I understand that you often go without stockings and do not even wear corsets."

Crissa stared in astonishment. "But women have not worn corsets for years." Then, noticing her aunt's figure, she realised her mistake at once. "That is, I mean, young . . ." She felt herself flushing and broke off a piece of bread to hide her confusion.

Aunt Clara's voice held chill resignation. "So I was correct last evening. It might well be your mother sitting there. You have the same regrettable red hair, the same wilful mouth and bold eyes. You appear also to have inherited her argumentativeness which so embarrassed your poor father, and the same lack of respect for your elders that she exhibited towards me."

Crissa pushed back her chair and rose. "Aunt Clara, I cannot listen to you any longer. Your age and relationship give you the right to reprimand or criticise *me*. But I will not tolerate these insults to my mother."

Across the dining table they faced each other. Crissa caught sight of herself in the gilt-framed mirror, saw that the green flecks in her eyes showed clearly, that her cheeks were unnaturally red. Miss Conway behaved exactly as her brother would have done. She tightened her mouth, pinched in her nostrils and spoke in a clipped, emotionless tone.

"You and Henrietta will be ready to accompany me at exactly ten o'clock."

As she went stiffly from the room, Crissa gripped the table edge, feeling a strong temptation to hurl half the Derby breakfast set across the room.

"Hell fire!" She uttered with guilty satisfaction

the oath she had learned from Harry, and repeated it several times, forcefully and aloud.

Hearing a sound from the doorway she put her hands to her flushed cheeks and swung round in dismay. The young French officer was eyeing her with interest and admiration. She bent her head as he came forward and bowed.

"You are a little *distraite*, mademoiselle? It is *le dragon*, is it not? She has quite cast out the pleasure I perceived on your face when you looked out of the window earlier this morning."

"It was really my own fault," Crissa admitted hastily. "I fear I provoked her."

He shrugged dismissively. "That is so easily done. Miss Conway is a—how do you say?—worthy lady, no doubt. But there are so many things of which she does not approve."

"You find that also, Monsieur de Beauvoir?"

He smiled sympathically. "But of course. You must not allow her to upset you. You should always be happy, mademoiselle. It is your nature to be so, I am sure."

Crissa looked at him from beneath lowered lashes. "You cannot possibly know my nature."

He bent a little towards her. "In that you are mistaken. When I saw you for the first time yesterday, it was as if the sun had come out on so grey and doleful a day. Your hair shone so brightly against the dark trees . . ."

"I was wearing a poke bonnet," she pointed out.

The young man burst out laughing. "Ah, you catch me out! But you will forgive a small untruth? For in all sincerity, mademoiselle, I greatly welcome the presence of yourself and your sister in this house. I suppose I should be grateful that I am not shut up in the depot at Princetown where, I am told, life for many of my countrymen is only one degree better than on the hulks. But"—he spread his hands—"you will appreciate, I am sure, that it is not easy for a man of spirit to live such a restricted and useless life. There is little to occupy one's energy in this isolated place."

"Is that why you were digging in the garden?" Crissa enquired with sudden intuition. "Not because you were made to?"

He drew himself up. "I cannot be made to do anything, mademoiselle, save keep to the conditions of my parole." He repeated them like a child reciting a carefully learned poem. "I may walk one mile along the turnpike road in the direction of the town only. I must be inside this house by eight o'clock in summer, five o'clock in winter. I must report to the prisoners' agent in Tavistock twice a week, and submit to him every letter that I write." Again he shrugged. "But we officers on parole should not complain. Mostly people are sympathetic towards us. In fact, there are those in Tavistock, it is rumoured, who will organise . . ." He broke off abruptly. "But no, it is not good that you should know of such things."

Crissa glanced at the clock. "Forgive me, monsieur, but I must go upstairs now and warn my sister to get ready to go out. Aunt Clara insists that we accompany her to Tavistock this morning."

"You are walking there?" he asked. When she nodded, he said eagerly, "You will permit me to ask Miss Conway if I may accompany you? I must go to the town in any case, to collect the allowance your generous government grants me. You would not object to my company?"

She glanced at him appraisingly. He was certainly as handsome a man as she had ever met. She judged him a little older than herself, and he was obviously as much a misfit in this house as she was. There was something else she saw also; the nervous energy pent up inside him, which struck a chord of sympathy within herself.

"I would not have the least objection, sir," she assured him, and was gratified to see his face light up with pleasure.

She was half-way upstairs, and Monsieur de Beauvoir had already disappeared when she recalled that Hetty would be with them. Her spirits sank at that thought. Between Aunt Clara's open disapproval of herself and Hetty's antagonism to the young Frenchman, the walk which could have been so pleasant seemed to offer nothing but constraint and difficulties.

In the event, only two set out, she and Aunt Clara. Hetty had fainted again and appeared so unwell that grudgingly she had been excused. As for the young man, his offer to accompany them had been firmly set aside. Crissa, dressed in a pale lemon muslin gown with a pelisse of greenish yellow velvet and a feather-trimmed bonnet, heard his voice coming from the porch as she crossed the hall.

"But, Mademoiselle Conway, I could protect you from any dangers you might encounter upon the road."

Aunt Clara's acid tones answered him. "I do not remember your being concerned about any such dangers previously, Monsieur de Beauvoir. Your sudden anxiety upon my behalf appears to coincide with my niece's arrival, but I assure you I am quite capable of determining that she comes to no harm during her stay here."

As Crissa joined them, the Frenchman cast her a crestfallen glance. He bowed formally to them both, then turned on his heel. As he disappeared down the leaf-strewn drive, Aunt Clara pinched in her nostrils in the way that was becoming familiar to her niece.

"That young man sometimes fails to appreciate his good fortune. He might quite easily be lodged in some tiny room in a back street instead of in the house of an acquaintance of his family."

And would probably be a good deal happier there, Crissa thought to herself. But for the moment she was relieved to find her aunt's disapproval directed elsewhere. As they set out for the town, she looked about her with interest.

As soon as they left the drive she felt the keen air off the moor. The sun still shone in a cloudless sky, lighting up the bracken and heather upon the far slopes, reflecting the brilliant gorse blossoms. She could see sheep grazing, and ponies high up amongst the tumbled rocks of the tors. On such a morning the moor looked a place of peace, and it was impossible to believe Phoebe's stories of evil spirits, of men being lured to their deaths by voices which were not human; of haunted places where not even the bravest would venture alone. Glancing at her aunt, walking beside her with upright carriage and stern face, one hand gripping the handle of a large umbrella, Crissa doubted if even supernatural beings would have the power to daunt this elderly spinster. She noted, as they reached the outskirts of the town, that her aunt was greeted on all sides with the greatest deference, and she was reminded of the old lady's reference to their family being highly regarded in the district for generations. And just as she had felt some sympathy for her father's attitude until he revealed his callous plan for removing Hetty's child, so now Crissa suddenly perceived that there was some justification for her aunt's censorious behaviour. After all, Hetty *had* got herself with child, even though she had married the father immediately it was known. And Peter Stanhope had already been refused permission even to pay court to her. Although Crissa's heart ached for her young sister in the tragedy which had followed her ill-advised behaviour, she could not but recognise how wicked that behaviour must seem to a woman of Aunt Clara's stamp. It was, she saw clearly, her own task to attempt some mediation between Hetty and Aunt Clara. To that end, she resolved once more to repress her own rebellious thoughts.

She remarked pleasantly, "It appears to be a very well kept town, ma'am."

"That is largely due to the Duke of Bedford who owns most of it," Aunt Clara informed her. "Tavistock is a very old town. Over there, near to the church, you may see the ruins of the Benedictine Abbey."

Crissa, however, was more interested in the people about her than in ancient ruins. Especially as mingling with the prosperous looking townspeople and farmers were a great many French officers. Even had she not heard their quick, animated talk she would have marked them out at once as different. Many of them were young and handsome. They laughed and gestured a great deal and were altogether more lively than the local men. She saw their heads turn as she passed, their admiring glances. But seeing the warning look on Aunt Clara's face, she demurely bent her head and kept her gaze directed downwards as became a modest young woman of good family.

Not even Aunt Clara could complain of her behaviour as she accompanied the old lady through the town, waiting patiently in the various shops, carrying small purchases, solicitously offering an arm when the road surface became uneven. She was unexpectedly rewarded.

"I am going to pay a call upon a friend who is indisposed," Aunt Clara informed Crissa when her shopping was completed. "She will not wish to entertain a stranger at present. I will show you where you may wait for me in some seclusion."

She led the way to the Abbey Bridge and from the parapet pointed to a bench set against a high wall a few yards along the riverside path.

"I shall enjoy sitting there in the sun," Crissa said with enthusiasm. "There is a charming view."

Aunt Clara glanced at her watch. "I shall be gone precisely twenty minutes, Clarissa. During that time you will not move from that seat, nor speak to anyone. Do you understand?"

It could have been her father speaking. "I understand, ma'am," she said resignedly. And added for good measure, "I hope you will find your friend much improved."

She sighed with relief as she strolled towards the

seat. It was exceedingly pleasant here by the river. The high wall sheltered her from the fresh breeze and the sun's warmth spread through her whole body. She unbuttoned her pelisse and leaning her head against the wall, closed her eyes and listened to the lively water music of the weir.

A familiar voice broke into her reverie. "Shall I disturb you if I sit here beside you?"

She straightened abruptly and looked with alarm at the laughing face of the French prisoner.

"Oh, no, please, Monsieur de Beauvoir. My aunt will be so angry if she discovers you here. She gave me the strictest instructions that I was to speak to no one."

He bent towards her conspiratorially. "Did she say how long she would be gone?"

"Twenty minutes exactly."

"Then we are safe enough. Miss Conway is a lady of fixed habits, and a stickler for time. She is never a minute earlier or later than she states. You may rely on it." His blue eyes regarded her with amusement. "You will not try to make me believe, mademoiselle, that you have never made assignations that were not a trifle indiscreet? Or broken a rule or two, and sometimes disobeyed your nurse or governess? The other one now—your sister—she, I can well believe, would be obedient, a little nervous perhaps of being otherwise. But not you. We are two of a kind, Mademoiselle Clarissa. I knew that the moment I met you."

Crissa drew slightly away from him. "That is the second time you have taken upon yourself to assess my character, monsieur. It is not very polite."

"But intriguing, you will allow?" He leaned back,

negligently crossing one elegantly booted leg over the other. "I have discovered there is nothing pleases a woman so much as conversation which turns upon herself."

"And you are, I surmise, vastly experienced in the art of pleasing women?"

He smiled at her, revealing perfectly shaped teeth. "Naturally. Although it may sound a little boastful, I have had only one failure."

"Indeed?"

"It was, I think, a very natural one. The lady in question being *le dragon*—your aunt." He made a wry face and Crissa laughed.

"I do not think Aunt Clara would respond to compliments."

Idly he flicked at the tassel of his boot. "She is strange, that one. My English *grandmère* is strict, but not like that. Sometimes I think Miss Conway has acid in her veins instead of good red blood. I thought that all women had some kindness in their hearts, however much they may choose to hide it for their own purposes. I can be termed an enemy of your country, certainly. At least," he added ruefully, "I could when I was in my ship. Now I am at the mercy of your countrymen. And mostly they are kind to me. Why, then, should Mademoiselle Conway, who professes to take a special interest in me, act so coldly?"

"I do not think you should take her attitude so personally, Monsieur de Beauvoir. It is her nature, as my mother discovered long ago, to be cold and —and disapproving. I think perhaps she cannot help it. But I cannot believe it makes for any happiness."

The young man traced a pattern on the path with

the toe of his boot. "Is she also unkind to the little one—your sister?"

"Aunt Clara has scarce spoken more than a dozen words to Hetty."

"She is indisposed this morning?"

"She is very tired after our journey," Crissa told him cautiously.

"When I carried her upstairs last evening, I could not fail to observe . . . she is *enciente, n'est-ce-pas?*"

Crissa turned quickly away. "Monsieur de Beauvoir, in France such a subject may be considered suitable for conversation between a gentleman and a lady. I do assure you it is not so in this country."

He bent low to look up at her face, hidden by her bonnet. His eyes were troubled. "Forgive me. I had no wish to embarrass you. But your sister looked so—so unhappy. When she first saw me she seemed startled, frightened almost. I could not understand why I should affect her in that way. Or perhaps," he added, as if trying to convince himself, "she was already feeling faint, and that was why she turned away from me."

Crissa clasped her gloved fingers tightly together. How could she tell this young man who seemed to her charming and agreeable—considerably more so than some young Englishmen of her acquaintance —that Hetty was consumed with hatred against him and all his compatriots? Seeing him gazing at her, with the puzzled hurt of a child whose friendly advances have been repulsed, she was more than ever certain that even were she in Hetty's shoes, she could not feel her sister's bitter antagonism towards the whole French nation.

She said, "My sister *is* very unhappy, sir. Her

husband died not many weeks ago. And you are right. Her child is due in three months."

His eyes were as dismayed as his tone. "*Oh, la pauvre petite.* I am so sorry, mademoiselle. She is too young for such sorrow."

"Yes," Crissa agreed sadly. "She is but eighteen."

He sat silent for some moments, his hands clasped between his knees. Then he asked, "How long are you to stay at Grimstone House?"

"Until . . . about four months, I think."

He looked at her in astonishment. "She is to have her baby there?"

Crissa nodded, wishing he would not ask so many questions, yet at the same time feeling some relief in finding so sympathetic a confidant.

She chose her words carefully. "Hetty is not strong. My father considered that the moorland air would benefit her. And our mother having died some years ago, you see, he thought that Aunt Clara . . ." She floundered to a stop, hearing the lack of conviction in her voice.

Monsieur de Beauvoir shook his head. "No, mademoiselle, that is not the reason. But already I have asked too many questions. For that I beg your pardon. I trespass, I think, on forbidden ground and I will not embarrass you further. Only I have great pity for *la pauvre* Hetty." His face brightened. "At least, there is one consolation."

"What is that?"

"Your sister will have the best medical care anyone could wish for. Dr. Leland, who is a good friend of mine, is a most skilled and dedicated physician. In fact, sometimes I think he is not aware there is anything more in life than his work and a pipe of tobacco. It is not good for a man, that." He slapped his knee, making Crissa start. "Why, talk of the devil! Here he is, Paul Leland himself."

Crissa looked where he pointed, along the path to their right. A man was walking slowly towards them, a tall, broad-shouldered man dressed in light buckskin trousers and dark blue coat with a velvet collar. He was carrying his beaver hat and his head was bent so that she could not see his face. His hair was black and curly like a water poodle's. He was so deep in thought that the Frenchman had to hail him twice before he halted and jerked up his head. Then, to her dismay, Crissa recognised the horseman with whom she had had such an unpleasant encounter the previous day. She heard her companion making the introductions. She inclined her head, murmured a greeting. But in her mind a thought was taking shape. This man, whom Hetty had so antagonised, would deliver her baby. He, who had so openly shown sympathy for Napoleon's troops, would be the first to take in his hands the child of Peter Stanhope who had been killed by the guns of a French privateer.

It was absurd even to entertain that idea, she told herself. There must be another doctor in the town. Besides, she could not imagine Aunt Clara employing so young a physician. For now that she saw him bareheaded, the grim appearance of yesterday banished as he greeted his friend, she realised that he was younger than she had supposed—still under thirty, she guessed.

Armand de Beauvoir, apparently oblivious to the coldness between his companions, was cheerfully explaining the situation.

"Am I not fortunate, Paul? See what *le bon Dieu* has sent to brighten my exile! A charming young lady who has an equally beautiful sister. They are nieces of Miss Conway, though you can scarce credit that, can you?"

"You are staying at Grimstone House?" the doctor enquired without the least inflection of interest in his voice.

"For a few months," Crissa answered in an equally indifferent tone.

"And Mademoiselle Clarissa and I will contrive, I am sure, to meet occasionally despite the all-seeing eye of *le dragon*."

Dr. Leland asked with a superior air, "What makes you suppose this lady will be anxious to meet you, Armand?"

The young man looked taken aback. "*Eh bien*, because . . ." Perplexity in his eyes, he turned to Crissa. "If I embarrass you, mademoiselle, I ask your forgiveness. But your manner, if I may be so bold as to say so, gave me no indication that my company was distasteful to you."

"Neither is it," Crissa assured him swiftly. "Your presence, on the other hand, will make my stay at Grimstone more tolerable."

The doctor's tone was sarcastic. "I see. Monsieur de Beauvoir being an officer, and a particularly handsome young man to boot, makes a difference to your attitude?"

Crissa rose, her cheeks burning. "You have no right to speak to me in this manner, sir. Rather do you owe me an apology since your spur badly marked our carriage yesterday. Besides which you were churlish in the extreme. I was never spoken to like that ..."

"No, I do not suppose you were," he interrupted her imperturbably. "I surmise that Armand is but one of many young men who pay you pretty compliments—both you and your sister. But when you block a turnpike road ..."

Armand laid a hand on his friend's arm. "Paul, I implore you. Do not upbraid Miss Conway in this manner. I have no notion what your quarrel may be about, but she is upset enough already with—with one thing and another. It is most ungallant of you to add to her distress."

Crissa was aware of the older man's eyes on her, swiftly appraising her from her gay bonnet to her white kid ankle boots.

"I am sorry if Miss Conway is distressed," he said coolly. "But I think I may be forgiven for failing to observe that to be the case." He smiled at the Frenchman but it was not a pleasant smile. "Doubtless you are able to offer her consolation, Armand. After all, you are more practised in that art than I am."

His friend's face grew even more perplexed. "What has happened to you this moring, Paul?" Turning to Crissa, he went on quickly, "I assure you, mademoiselle, Dr. Leland is not usually so fierce and—and discourteous. Perhaps a patient has given you some anxiety, Paul? But of course, I must not ask that, for you will never speak of such matters. But *something* has angered you, and it is most ungentlemanly ..."

Crissa slipped the ribbon of her reticule over her wrist. "I assure you, Monsieur de Beauvoir, that

Dr. Leland's attitude is of no consequence to me."

"But—but it should be," Armand protested. "For do you not see? One day, Mademoiselle Hetty will . . ." He was silenced by her frown, but only for a moment. "He truly is a very kind man, mademoiselle. He is so good to all of us parole prisoners. He invites us to his house and . . ."

"Armand." The doctor's voice held a warning.

The young man, however, was determined to continue his defence of his friend. "No, do not stop me, Paul. It is good that Miss Clarissa knows that you have this other side." He turned to Crissa, eagerness in his face. "Why, he has such a reputation for helping us unfortunates that it is said that when a prisoner escapes, Dr. Leland's house should be the first to be searched."

The doctor's fingers closed on the younger man's wrist so that he winced. "Armand, you let your tongue run away with you."

The Frenchman flushed. "I—I was but joking."

"Then you should take care in what company you make such jokes. It seems that you are unaware as yet that to Miss Clarissa Conway and her sister the only good Frenchman is a dead one. However sweetly she may smile upon you and pretend to enjoy your company, I assure you that her real feelings are quite different. She would have you and all your countrymen treated not like men, but vermin."

"How dare you!" Crissa exclaimed furiously. "If you had but listened yesterday, I could have explained that . . . Oh, dear," she broke off in dismay. "There is Aunt Clara. I must not be seen talking to you."

Both men glanced towards the bridge. Armand

said at once, "Turn your back upon Miss Conway, Paul. Forgive me, mademoiselle, for such discourtesy but it is for your own sake. Sit down and ignore us."

Crissa did as he bid her. He caught hold of the doctor's arm and led him protesting along the riverside path.

She called after him, "Thank you, Monsieur de Beauvoir. And pray believe . . ." But he was out of hearing.

On the homeward walk Crissa was again a model of decorum. But this time it was because she was concerned with her own thoughts, and those thoughts had no connection with Aunt Clara or Hetty or her own frustrations. She was wondering just how much Paul Leland would reveal to Armand and how much the young man would believe of the doctor's account of yesterday's unpleasant interlude. If he did believe his friend's version, he would be hurt, she was sure, hurt by her supposed antipathy to all his countrymen, and by what he must judge the falseness of her friendly attitude towards him. She did not want him hurt. She did not want him to think badly of her. What she did desire was to face that hateful doctor with a battery of all the strongest words in her vocabulary and let fly at him until lack of breath forced her to stop. And then turn on her heel and march away.

As she and Aunt Clara parted on the landing, the old lady remarked tartly, "I am gratified to perceive that my words have had some effect, Clarissa. Both you and your sister have very obviously suffered from a lack of restraint. I shall do my utmost to correct that while you are here. I trust you will find Henrietta sufficiently recovered to join us for luncheon."

Hetty in fact was a great deal better. She greeted Crissa sympathetically. "Was it dreadful for you, dear? Did she criticise you *all* the way?" Before her sister could reply, she continued with her questions. "What is the town like? Is there likely to be any social life at all? And did you meet anyone of interest?"

Crissa, who was used to confiding all her activities to Hetty, was about to tell her of her encounters. Then, suddenly remembering her sister's attitude to Armand, changed her mind.

"Do you suppose I was allowed to meet anyone at all?" she asked, making a face. "The town is tolerable enough. You would not suppose it to be a mining town, it is so well kept. I am told there is much copper found in these parts and some talk of using the French prisoners of war to help build a canal to carry the metal to Morwellham Quay some four miles away."

"That is what they should be put to," Hetty exclaimed, and again Crissa's heart sank at the harshness in her voice. It seemed that she would have to guard against even the mention of a Frenchman if a supposedly harmless remark on her part was to be met with such bitterness.

Phoebe, taking Crissa's coat, asked in a whisper, "Can I speak to you alone, please, miss?"

Crissa followed the maid into the little dressing closet which served as Phoebe's bedroom.

"What is it?" she asked. "You look worried."

"I am that, Miss Clarissa, there's no denying. I've

done something I shouldn't 'ave but I'm glad I did. You'll not be angry with me?"

"How can I say until you have told me?"

The maid hung Crissa's pelisse in the wardrobe. "I've been eavesdropping, that's what." When she turned back to Crissa, her face was puckered in anxiety. "Not that I meant to, ma'am," she added earnestly. "But I was just going into the kitchen to get some milk for Miss Hetty about mid-morning when I heard voices. One was Martha's—she being your aunt's old housekeeper that let us in yesterday, and a proper crotchety old faggot. Everything in her kitchen is kept under lock and key and measured out so careful I'd needs almost to beg for a second slice of bread to my breakfast."

"Get on with your story, Phoebe."

The maid looked offended. "I was just trying to explain how I come to be listening 'cos 'tis not my habit as you know. It was something Martha said as made me decide not to go into the kitchen at all. She said, 'There's trouble in this house and 'tis my belief you could help to rid us of it.' "

"To whom was she saying this?"

"A proper wicked-looking old crone, for I saw her afterwards going down the drive. And a queer voice she had, kind of cracked and whining. And *she* said, 'I suppose 'tis the baby that's the trouble?' And Martha asked her how she knew anything about Miss Hetty's baby, and the old woman made answer with these words, ma'am. 'There's ways I have of knowing things as you'm well aware. And not with my eyes and ears. What is it you want me to do, rid her of the child?' "

"Phoebe, you are making this up!" Crissa protested in alarm.

"Indeed I'm not, Miss Clarissa. And there's more to come."

"Tell me quickly, then, or I shall be late for luncheon and that will greatly displease Aunt Clara."

"Very well, ma'am. Martha said, 'You've the power of over-looking, so I'm told. 'Twould be for my mistress's sake. 'Tis all too much for her. And I'll make it worth your while.'"

Crissa said impatiently, "I have not the least notion what you are talking about. What is over-looking, pray?"

"Why, 'tis the evil eye."

"Do not be ridiculous, Phoebe. No one believes in that nowadays."

"Don't they, then?" The maid bridled. Her expression grew stubborn. "I do, for one. And I reckon any that's country bred, especially folks who live close to the moor, wouldn't say 'twas ridiculous. There's plenty of cases I could tell you about. Cows that stopped giving milk for no reason. Little pigs that dropped down dead though they were running about as merry as you like a moment afore. And children taken ill with pains no doctor could account for. That's what over-looking means, ma'am, and 'tis black witches as have the power of it in their wicked eyes."

Crissa turned towards the door. "I am not going to listen any longer. At first I was foolish enough to believe you might have heard of some real threat to Hetty. But this is simply superstition. And you see where your eavesdropping has led you. This fancy that some old woman can harm Hetty's baby by power of her eye is all of a piece with your story of Lady Howard's coach and its headless driver, and those silly wish hounds you are so afraid of. You are not to repeat one word of this to Miss Hetty, do you understand?"

The girl's face set even more obstinately. "Whether I speak of it or not won't make a mite of difference. That old witch will over-look Miss Hetty for sure unless she can be stopped. And 'tis only us can stop her. If you won't even believe me, that just leaves me."

For the rest of that day Crissa dismissed Phoebe's warning from her mind. Yet that night, lying wakeful beside Hetty in the big feather bed, it came back to her.

She had known well enough that this banishment to Grimstone House would be a trying time for both of them. But it seemed now that difficulties she had not foreseen were besetting her on all sides. Both she and Hetty had antagonised the doctor who would possibly deliver Hetty's child. Under the same roof during the rest of her sister's pregnancy would be an officer of the hated French navy, accentuating Hetty's grief and bitterness over her husband's death. And now their maid had developed this superstitious fancy. To cap it all, Aunt Clara had delivered an hour long lecture to Hetty on the wickedness of her ways, and it had taken Crissa almost as long to stem her sister's tears and soothe her to sleep. The one gleam of brightness might already have been extinguished, if Armand de Beauvoir had believed Dr. Leland's story. For was her own denial likely to carry weight against the words of a man for whom the Frenchman had so marked a respect and admiration?

It was a still night and the window shutters had not been closed. Crissa lay staring at the sky through the lattice, wishing she were in Dartmouth, that in a moment she would hear a pebble softly hit the pane, thrown by Harry whose laughing face would be upturned to greet her when she opened her window.

She could no longer lie still. Easing herself carefully out of bed, she pulled her dressing-gown around her shoulders and tiptoed across the bare floor. The room smelt damp and stuffy. Cautiously she lifted the latch and opened the window. She had never accepted the dictum that the night air was dangerous. After all, did not sailors endure it, and the shepherds at lambing time? Often at home, without the added incentive of Harry's presence, she would stand at her window on moonlit nights, revelling in the beauty of the silvered river. There would be familiar, recognisable sounds: the soft lap of water against the stones of the quay, a creak of ropes; the squeak of rowlocks as a late party of sailors returned to their ship; shouting and laughter as another group emerged from the inn. Dogs barking at the disturbance, the whistling calls of oyster-catchers from the mudbanks. And on dark nights there would be lanterns bobbing along the streets and the friendly, reassuring lights which marked the ships at anchor.

Here there was nothing. Only the vast, empty quiet of the moor. The silence seemed to her so real, so mysteriously palpable that she quieted her own breathing as if she were committing an offence. What lay out there, beyond the drive, beyond the dark river in the valley? What happened at night, with only the silver of moon and a scattering of stars to see? Were there really supernatural beings roaming that wild rock-strewn tract of upland, as Phoebe so fervently believed? Were there ghostly hands which beckoned the unwary traveller into bogs, and a phantom coach with a white-faced occupant doomed for ever to travel nightly the road Crissa could just glimpse through the trees? And were there really wish hounds and . . . ?

She caught her breath and drew back, a hand at her mouth, as a wild, mournful howl came from far across the moor. She waited, scarcely daring to breathe. The sound was repeated, unearthly in the lonely silence.

Crissa closed the window and slipped quickly back into bed. Her cold fingers felt for Hetty's hand and clasped it. The sound, of course, had been the whining of some farm dog as wakeful in the night as she was. So she told herself. But she was only half convinced.

3

It was Aunt Clara's custom, Crissa discovered, to retire to a little parlour after breakfast each morning and there spend half an hour dealing with household accounts and correspondence. This was the time Armand chose, knowing he would be safe from her critical eye, to occupy himself in the overgrown garden. It seemed to Crissa an excellent opportunity to learn what his future attitude to her would be.

His greeting gave her some reassurance. But, after all, he *was* French and Frenchmen had a reputation for charm; and in many cases, insincerity. For a few minutes they exchanged polite conversation, he complimenting her on her appearance, she praising the improvements he had made in the flower borders. Then, seating herself on a granite bench where she was hidden from the house by a hedge of clipped beech, she said tentatively, "Monsieur de Beauvoir, I believe I owe you an explanation."

He leaned on his fork, his blue eyes regarding her in the friendliest manner. "I am not aware of it, mademoiselle. As I said yesterday, the affair of your sister is . . ."

"I did not mean that. I was referring to—to certain remarks made by Dr. Leland regarding my attitude . . ."

"To my countrymen?" He frowned down at the turned earth. "Yes, that I did not understand. You had appeared so kind, so charming. But then I remembered that your sister had turned her back on me and . . ."

"Will you allow me to explain—please? Dr. Leland had some justification for his remarks."

He shook his head. "No, mademoiselle. There could be no justification for a gentleman to speak to a lady in that manner. I could scarcely believe my ears."

"Did he tell you what occurred on the Plymouth road?"

Again he shook his head vehemently. "No. And if he had, I would not have listened. But I will listen to you, with the greatest pleasure. You will permit me to sit beside you?"

He scraped his boots and brushed some earth from his trousers. Crissa moved along the seat to make room for him. He made no comment until she had finished her explanation, but she saw his face grow troubled.

"So you see," she ended, finding it much easier than she had anticipated, "there is a reason, however ill-judged, for Hetty's antagonism. But I do ask you to believe, whatever Dr. Leland's opinion, that I do not share it."

"Of course I will believe you." He took hold of her hand. "And I understand perfectly about *la pauvre petite* Hetty. It is no wonder she cannot bear the sight of me. I promise you, I will keep out of her way."

"You are very understanding," Crissa murmured, knowing she should draw her hand away from his, yet reluctant to do so.

"Must we not try to understand each other?" he asked, his fingers caressing her wrist. "One day this war will be ended, and we cannot go on being enemies for ever. It has two sides, war. For those of us who go to fight, it is an adventure—until we get wounded or captured. But for those we leave behind, our wives and sweethearts, mothers, and sisters . . ."

"You have a wife in France?" Crissa asked, and found the idea not at all to her liking.

"I am not married, nor even betrothed," he answered to her relief. "But for my mother and sisters, it is not a happy time. Worse for my *grand-mère* since she is English and her loyalties must be divided. Perhaps you, mademoiselle have someone very dear to you, fighting in Europe?"

"There are a number of young men of my acquaintance, and my cousin Nicholas . . ."

"But there is no one for whom you would break your heart, like your poor sister?"

"Not yet," she answered lightly. "Though there is a young gentleman in Dartmouth who professes to . . ."

"Naturally," he said, smiling. "There must be many young men who have lost their hearts to you, Mademoiselle Clarissa. In fact, I cannot think how any man with natural feelings could fail to be instantly your devoted admirer!"

It was high time, she decided, that she showed a little decorum. She withdrew her hand from his grasp.

"You pay charming compliments, monsieur. But I can name at least one man who is certainly not my admirer—Dr. Leland."

"Paul?" He frowned. "He is not a man who finds it easy to talk to ladies. In fact, I do not think he likes them on the whole. Something happened, years ago, which made him—what is the word?—bitter. He is a man who gives freely of himself to his patients, sparing little time for entertainment or pleasure of any kind. There was a young woman, I think, who did not understand this, and who wanted him always at her beck and call. There was a quarrel —and—but no, he would not like me to speak of it. The little I *have* said will perhaps help you to understand why he was so angry when you stopped him going to the French prisoners. They were hurt. They needed him. And you and your sister were in his way. It is a pity that you three have taken such a dislike to each other. For you will need him one day, will you not?"

"Is there no other doctor who could attend my sister?"

Armand shrugged. "Yes. But he is so old and slow that the baby would be cutting its teeth by the time he arrived. I do not think he acts any longer as *accoucheur*. I think you have no choice, mademoiselle. But do not be anxious. Paul will not let his feelings hold sway at such a time." His face cleared. "I will explain to him . . ."

"No." Realising how sharply she had spoken, Crissa added quickly, "It is kind of you, but I would prefer that you did not do so. An explanation was due to *you* after Dr. Leland's hurtful words yesterday. I do not consider it necessary to make any to him. And now that I have told you the truth, monsieur," she added, rising, "it is time I left you to continue with your task. It was, in any case, most indiscreet of me to seek you out. If Aunt Clara should hear of it . . ."

"She will breathe fire, and lock you in your room for the rest of the day? Poor Miss Clarissa. Poor Miss Hetty. Life will not be very gay for you in the next few months. If there is any service I can render you, within the limits of my parole, you have only to ask."

"Thank you. I will remember your offer, Monsieur de Beauvoir. Life cannot be very happy for you either, so far from your home and family. You receive letters from them?"

"Oh, yes, regularly. They are very good to me and send money. Your Government's allowance of eight shillings and ninepence a week does not go very far, especially with my taste in clothes and my liking for a bottle of wine. When I was in hospital they . . ."

"You were wounded?"

The young man drew himself up. "Naturally, mademoiselle. You do not suppose I would otherwise have allowed myself to be captured? I had a gunshot wound in my shoulder. When the English boarding party came over the side I could not use my sword. It did not occur to me until too late that I could have attempted a thrust with the left hand."

Crissa had a picture of him, lying bleeding on the deck, his blue eyes clouded with pain and frustration as he waited for death or the ignominy of capture.

She smiled at him and asked gently, "You are quite recovered now?"

"Perfectly. And my recovery is greatly due to Paul." He put a hand to his right shoulder. "Sometimes it pains me a little when the weather is cold and damp as it so often is here. But I can use my arm well enough as you see."

"And have you never tried to escape?"

He held himself erect, his shoulders thrust back, head high. He was no longer smiling, and the tone of his voice startled her. "Mademoiselle, I think you do not understand. I am an officer on parole. It is required that we give our word of honour not to attempt to escape, and to conduct ourselves in a manner proper to a gentleman. I would not step one yard off the turnpike road or beyond my limit of a mile, nor be out five minutes after the curfew bell has sounded. However difficult these rules are to keep, I have given my promise to do so."

"I beg your pardon," Crissa said contritely. "As you say, I did not fully understand. We have no prisoners of war in Dartmouth."

At once he was smiling again, his eyes bright. "Am I then the first Frenchman you have met?"

When she agreed, he asked teasingly, "And I am not as frightening as you had perhaps been led to suppose?"

"I do not find you frightening in the least, monsieur. In fact . . ."

"Yes?" He bent towards her expectantly.

She turned away. "You may guess what I was about to say," she told him provocatively over her shoulder.

He made to follow her, then stopped abruptly. Approaching them along the garden path was Hetty, dressed in a white gown and a blue silk cloak. At sight of them she pulled this more closely about her and would have turned back.

Armand stepped quickly forward. "Do not distress yourself, madame. I will not embarrass you with my company. Stay in the garden, I pray you. It will benefit you to take some exercise in the sun."

Hetty's back was rigid, but she had hesitated at Armand's words. Then she turned to them, her head bent, the brim of her bonnet hiding her face. Her answer seemed forced from her.

"Thank you. My sister has doubtless informed you why it is not possible for me to—to . . ."

"Endure my presence? Yes. And I understand perfectly." He bowed with elegant formality. "I bid you good-day, madame, mademoiselle."

When he had gone, Crissa said, "Hetty, I wish you did not feel such resentment. He is such a charming and altogether agreeable young man."

"And you have fallen in love with him already?"

Crissa held on to her patience, reminding herself again that her sister must be humoured. "I have done no such thing. But I enjoy talking to him, and he is not without his own problems."

"They are of his own making, in that he serves that fiend Napoleon who is the cause of all this misery."

Crissa was about to argue; then with relief noticed something which provided an excuse for changing the subject.

"How did you come by the posy you are wearing? It is a very odd one, to be sure."

Hetty fingered the spray of quickbeam interlaced with trefoil. "Phoebe made it for me. She says certain plants have some efficacy for anyone in my state."

"I have never heard tell of that before."

"The girl is full of old wives' tales as you know well enough." Hetty glanced with distaste at the posy. "I do not consider it very pretty but I wear it to humour her. It appears she went out early this morning especially to gather it, so I could not do otherwise, could I?"

Crissa linked her arm in her sister's. This was the Hetty she knew, so careful never to hurt another's feelings, even those of a maidservant.

"Do you feel equal to a turn in the garden? I

think it would be wise to take some exercise now, since I understand Aunt Clara has planned a morning's sewing for us while she reads from some edifying books."

Hetty looked dismayed. "Oh, dear. For my benefit, of course? The trouble is, Crissa, that I still do not feel wicked, only dreadfully unhappy. But I have brought such trouble upon Papa and Aunt Clara, and upon you as well. So I suppose I must be."

Crissa pressed her arm. "I do not consider you so. And even if you were, you are paying for it a hundredfold."

The younger girl halted and faced her sister, her eyes troubled. "But there is no reason why you should also suffer."

"There is one very good reason, dearest. That is because I love you more than any other person in the world." She bent forward and kissed her sister lightly on the cheek. "Now let us explore the garden. Who knows? We may discover some of Phoebe's pixies hiding under a gorse bush, for she would have us believe that Dartmoor is highly populated with such fascinating creatures."

By Sunday the bright weather still held and the two girls put on pale muslin gowns and silk cloaks to walk to church. As they were about to set out, Phoebe, with an exclamation of dismay, rushed upstairs. When she came hurrying down again she was carrying the posy of quickbeam and trefoil which she pinned hastily at Hetty's shoulder.

Miss Conway, joining them at that moment, remarked bitingly, "You do not suppose I shall allow you to wear that ridiculous bunch of weeds, do you, Henrietta? Take it off at once."

"Phoebe will be so hurt, ma'am. She gathered it especially."

Aunt Clara, her high bonnet making her even taller, glared at her niece. "Since when have you considered a maidservant's wishes before those of your elders? You will obey me at once or stay at home. And do not suppose, in that case, to do as you please for I should set you a fitting sermon to study and question you about it upon my return."

With a helpless glance at Phoebe, Hetty removed the posy. As Aunt Clara went towards the door, the maid grabbed the tattered bunch and hid it beneath her cloak.

"I'll find some way, that I will," she muttered as she followed in the wake of her young mistress with a flushed and anxious face.

Once they had settled in the family pew, Crissa made sure that Aunt Clara's attention was safely on her hymn book and glanced with interest around the church. The shopkeepers and their families looked well dressed and prosperous, which suggested they did well from supplying the needs of the French prisoners, both the officers in the town and the less fortunate inmates of the depot at Princetown. She was surprised to see so few Frenchmen until she remembered that most of them would be Papists.

She was surreptitiously peeping from beneath her bonnet along the pews opposite when she discovered that she herself was being studied, by Paul Leland. But immediately his eyes met hers he dropped his gaze to his hymn book. Just for that brief moment, however, she thought she had seen on his face a look which was not totally hostile. It gave her an unexpected little thrill of pleasure to recognise in that look the interest which she was accustomed to see in men's eyes. Not that it mattered in the least, she assured herself with a mental shrug, how Dr. Leland regarded her, save on Hetty's account.

Hetty, she saw, had not noticed his presence. In fact the younger girl, sitting beside their aunt, seemed totally absorbed in the service. But Phoebe gave her mistress a nudge and half-pointed to the doctor which earned her a frown from Crissa.

As they came out of church, Aunt Clara stopped to speak to some friends. When she made no move to introduce her nieces, they strolled down the path, Phoebe in their wake. Suddenly an old woman dressed in faded black with a tattered shawl over her head bobbed up from behind the low wall separating the churchyard from a narrow alley. Hetty was looking in the other direction but the maidservant cried out in dismay. She stepped in front of Hetty and, with the posy held out before her, made the sign of the cross.

There was a moment's silence. Then a babble of excited voices broke out around them.

"What was she doing, then?" a farmer's stout wife demanded. "Using the evil eye on you?"

"Not on me," Phoebe answered, and her voice was trembling. "She was over-looking my young mistress."

The woman cast a speculative eye at Hetty, who seemed quite unaware of what was going on. She shook her fist at the old woman who was cowering behind the wall.

"Be off with you, old witch. God's holy ground is no place for you."

Hetty asked in perplexity, "What has happened? Why is everyone so angry with that poor old woman?"

Crissa took her sister's arm and urged her down the path. "It is just a quarrel between some local women, dear. Take no notice."

The younger girl hung back. "But, Crissa, look. That boy is going to throw a stone. Oh, pray stop him!"

It was neither Crissa nor Hetty who prevented the act. It was Dr. Leland, gripping the boy's wrist so fiercely that he yelped. He faced the farmer's wife and the little group of women around her, and his voice was taut with anger.

"Leave that poor creature. She's but a witless old woman without family or friends. She can do you no possible harm."

The stout woman stood her ground. "You'll not make us believe that, sir. There's things *she* can do, and all witches can, be they black or white, that you can't, with all your learning. She was putting the evil eye on the unborn child that's hid beneath that young lady's cloak. And if 'tis born alive it'll be thanks to the little maid's quick action, not any skill of yours."

Crissa saw his mouth tighten, the flush mount to his cheeks. Before he could reply, Aunt Clara came down the path.

"Clarissa, Henrietta, why are you loitering here? Is something amiss?"

The doctor said quickly, "Nothing that need cause you any concern, Miss Conway. Your nieces were unfortunately involved in an altercation between some townspeople. It is of no consequence, I assure you." As the farmer's wife was about to protest, he turned to her and muttered grimly, "Hold your tongue, woman."

As Aunt Clara, apparently satisfied with his explanation, shepherded the girls out of the gate, Crissa glanced back. Dr. Leland was talking to Phoebe and by the stubborn expression on her face it was obvious he was chiding her for her action.

"Surely that was the objectionable physician we encountered on our way here?" Hetty asked when they were out of hearing of their aunt.

"Yes. He lives and practises in Tavistock."

Hetty was silent for a moment. Then she said anxiously, "You do not suppose I shall be obliged to have him attend me at my lying-in? I should not like that at all. He seems always so angry."

"Lieutenant de Beauvoir assures me he is an excellent doctor," Crissa said, and immediately realised her mistake.

Hetty stopped and faced her. "Is that to be taken as a recommendation? Are we now to judge an Englishman by what a *Frenchman* says of him?"

Aunt Clara, a few paces ahead, turned. "I should be obliged if you would refrain from raising your voices. It is most unseemly. And I cannot imagine why you are not walking upon either side of me in a proper and dignified manner."

For once Crissa was grateful for their aunt's intervention. By the time they reached Grimstone House Hetty was so tired that Crissa suggested she put her feet up and rest till lunch time. To her surprise Aunt Clara made no objection, even adding that she intended to do the same. She seemed strangely abstracted for the rest of the day and retired to bed immediately after their evening meal. This, and the fact that Hetty did not refer to the incident in the churchyard or to Paul Leland, was a great relief to Crissa.

As they were preparing for bed Hetty uttered a startled exclamation.

"What is it?" asked Crissa in alarm.

"Do not look so anxious," Hetty said, smiling. "It was merely the baby kicking. The movement was so strong it took me by surprise."

"God be praised!" Phoebe exclaimed.

Crissa looked warningly at her and followed her into the little dressing closet. Phoebe picked up the tattered posy and threw it out of the window.

"That'll be needed no more," she said with satisfaction. " 'Tis the first glance of a witch as does the harm. And that I stopped, for sure. That's what the posy was for, Miss Clarissa, to catch the first glance, and being fashioned of quickbeam which is called witchwood, and trefoil which is the flower of the Holy Trinity, it worked."

"I have never heard such nonsense," Crissa declared. "Besides, you heard what Dr. Leland said. That old woman can do no harm whatsoever."

The maid's face held a smug satisfaction. "And *you* heard what the good wife said, ma'am. When Miss Hetty's baby is born alive, it'll be me she can thank, not him. If I hadn't done what I did she'd not have felt any movement, not tonight nor any night till her time comes round. Nothing you or the doctor says will make me believe otherwise, so 'tis no use you trying, miss."

Passing along the landing on their way down to breakfast next morning, the two girls heard Martha's voice in the hall.

"And mind you tell the doctor to hurry. 'Tis Miss Conway of Grimstone has need of him and not some pernickety creature as would call him for no more'n a finger ache."

It was Armand who answered her from the front door. "I will tell him, *certainement*. He will come at once, I know."

"Not that I've any faith in that young one," the old woman declared. "But seemingly Dr. Sawyer is past it now."

"That he is. And I assure you, Miss Conway will have much better treatment from Dr. Leland."

Crissa hurried downstairs. "What has happened, Martha?"

The old servant closed the front door. "You may well ask," she answered grimly. "Just what I thought would happen so soon as I saw you enter this hall last week. 'Twas just as if *she'd* come back to upset the mistress all over again."

"She? Whom do you mean?"

Martha tossed her head. "That flibbertigibbet mother of yours, that's who. I mind the day well when Master Thomas brought her here. 'Twas bad enough him taking a wife, him and the mistress being so close all those years. But to bring one like that, flouting her red hair and green eyes, clinging to Master Thomas' arm as if she'd wholly taken possession of him. After all Miss Clara'd done for him, too, stinting herself so's he could take up the law. And now, when he finds he can't control his daughters any more than he could his wife, what does he do but send them to my mistress to deal with? It's all too much for her, that's what it is."

"How dare . . . ?"

Hetty's gentle voice cut short Crissa's protest. "Is Miss Conway very unwell, Martha?"

"That she is, and 'tis all your fault. Why did it have to be you, so like Master Thomas as you be, as got into trouble? Why shouldn't it have been that one?" She pointed a trembling finger at Crissa.

Again Hetty silenced her sister. "Is there anything we can do for Aunt Clara? She is in bed?"

The old servant nodded. "And like to stay there."

"Then we had best go up to her," Hetty said, making for the stairs.

Martha, moving surprisingly quickly, forestalled her. "That you won't. You've done enough harm already, the pair of you. The sooner you're away from this house the better, and that Frenchie too. For if I know anything of your sort," again she glared at Crissa, "there'll be another packet of trouble there soon."

Crissa retorted angrily, "Martha, you may be concerned over Aunt Clara, but I will not tolerate . . ."

Hetty put a hand on her arm. "Let her be, dear. Martha understandably is anxious and upset. Let us go and have breakfast and afterwards we may find some way of being helpful."

Martha stared at her, thin eyebrows drawn together. Grudgingly she said, "If you've a mind to, there's aplenty you can do. For there's more than

I can manage with the kitchen-maid away to her sister's wedding."

"Very well," Hetty said in the same mild tone. "You may tell us in due course how we may be of use."

Crissa, following her sister into the dining-room, demanded, "How can you be so charitable, after Aunt Clara's treatment of us and the way that horrid old woman spoke of Mama?"

Hetty said patiently, "They are both old, Crissa, and it cannot be easy for them to have us here, particularly in the circumstances. Yesterday in church I thought a great deal about my behaviour. I see now that it was wicked. Papa trusted us both when he went away and I betrayed his trust. I could not help falling in love with Peter, but I should not have . . ." She paused, and Crissa saw the tears well into her eyes.

"But you did, Hetty, and that cannot be altered. And the church teaches us to forgive as well as condemn. There is no forgiveness in Papa's heart or Aunt Clara's. I cannot feel any real sympathy for her now. Nor do I suppose she is really unwell. She was perfectly all right yesterday."

"She did rest before luncheon and go early to bed." Hetty pointed out, beginning her breakfast.

Crissa gave an exaggerated shudder. "Ugh! Porridge! I dare say it was merely an excuse to loosen her corsets. Did you see how tightly she was laced?"

An hour late, she stood before Paul Leland in the drawing-room. To her surprise he had asked to see her when he had finished the examination of his patient.

"You are Miss Conway's nearest relative, I think?" he said, bowing perfunctorily.

"Except for my father."

"And he is—where?"

"At home in Dartmouth."

He stood before the window, hands clasped beneath his coat tails. After a few moments he turned and sat down opposite her. "Then I shall take the liberty of explaining to you the seriousness of your aunt's condition."

Crissa leaned forward. "Is she really ill, then?"

"She is suffering from a severe heart condition. With care she may survive for several years. But any shock or undue distress . . ." He shrugged, leaving the sentence unfinished.

Her hands felt cold. Guiltily she recalled her easy dismissal of Aunt Clara's indisposition, her facetious remarks.

"I had no idea of this. I am sure my father also is ignorant of her condition."

"I am scarcely surprised to hear that," he said coldly. "After all, you have not visited her for many years, have you? And when you choose to do so . . ."

"*Choose!* You do not suppose we . . . ?" She broke off, colouring under his critical look. "Did not Aunt Clara explain the position to you?"

"I have advised Miss Conway not to talk more than is absolutely necessary. She must be kept completely quiet."

"I see." Crissa bent her head, trying to take in the news he had given her. Then, facing him again, she said determinedly, "Since you appear to blame my sister and myself for my aunt's sudden indisposition, I would like to say that not by any word or action has she given us to understand she was other than completely well."

"That does not surprise me, either. Miss Conway is a lady of great courage and determination. I consider it likely she would entirely disapprove of my talking to you in this manner. But I felt you, as the person most responsible"—his tone was sarcastic—"should be made aware of the position."

She answered in a tone as biting as his. "Thank you, that was most kind. Do you think I should write and inform my father?"

He rose, picking up hat and whip. "Certainly. And I would suggest that you and your sister end your visit here as soon as convenient."

Crissa looked up at him in dismay. "But that is . . ." She rose and said with dignity, "I am afraid we cannot do so, sir, without my father's permission."

His eyebrows lifted slightly. "Then I would suggest you seek it without delay. The presence in this house of a French officer, however proper may be Lieutenant de Beauvoir's behaviour, coupled with that of you two young ladies, is not a situation I would recommend as being beneficial to Miss Conway's health."

Crissa retorted icily, "I notice you lay stress upon Lieutenant de Beauvoir's behaviour. The inference I draw is naturally that you are more doubtful of mine. I assume that because you came upon me sitting on a bench, unchaperoned . . ."

"You are mistaken, ma'am. I am not presuming to cast the slightest doubt upon your propriety. As for Armand, he is unquestionably a man of honour. But . . ."

"You two gentlemen should form a society for mutual admiration," she cut in. "But Monsieur de Beauvoir at least has some regard for *my* feelings."

"Which, considering your attitude towards his countrymen, is to his credit." Ignoring her protest, he went on coldly, "Doubtless you are well accustomed to receive men's admiration, Miss Conway. Whereas I do not for a moment deny that nature has endowed you with great beauty, I could wish that she had granted you also a more charitable disposition. My first meeting with you was marked by a display of extreme callousness on the part of your sister and yourself. Yesterday you made not the slightest attempt to prevent your maid provoking an ugly scene in which a harmless old woman would have been stoned but for my intervention. And this morning, Miss Conway's housekeeper was about to enter the dining-room to wait upon you when she was quite taken aback by your light-hearted attitude. I believe you even expressed the opinion that your aunt's indisposition was due to the tight lacing of her corsets." His bow was so slight as to be insulting. "For the moment I bid you good day, ma'am. I shall return this evening."

Crissa stood quite still for some minutes after she heard the thud of his horse's hooves fade away from down the drive. In twenty-one years only one man had ever addressed her in such a manner—her father. Her nails bit into the flesh of her palms; her cheeks were burning. The beating of her heart was so loud and hard that it quite frightened her. She counted aloud, slowly, keeping her eyes averted from the delicate Chinese vase on the pedestal table, which would splinter so easily into a thousand pieces to give vent to her anger.

By the time Hetty entered the room, anxious to know what had passed between her sister and the doctor, the only indication of Crissa's disturbed state was a tremor in her voice. And this, she realised with relief, Hetty would naturally attribute to the news she had just received regarding their aunt.

## 4

Aunt Clara lay back against the pillows, her face grey and gaunt, her hands limp on the sheet. But her mouth was set in its usual resolute line and her eyes had lost none of their sharpness.

"What did he say to you—that self-opinionated young man?"

"That you were to be kept quiet, and rest," Crissa answered, hoping she would not be questioned too closely.

"Did he tell you to write to your father?"

"I asked him if he thought it advisable," she replied cautiously.

"And he answered that you should?"

"I think he is right, ma'am. After all, Papa ought to be made aware . . ."

"I did not ask for your opinion, miss." The invalid turned her head and stared out of the window.

Crissa noted the sagging skin and deep lines; the

blue veins at the temples. A few strands of white hair showing beneath the plain unbecoming cap looked dull and lifeless. For the first time the significance of old age was borne in upon her. The body failing, nothing ahead to look forward to.

Impulsively she put out her hand and laid it over her aunt's. As if she had been stung, Aunt Clara snatched hers away. Her eyes were as hard as ever.

"I do not want your pity, Clarissa. I desire your obedience."

Crissa, flushing, bent her head. "Very well, ma'am. Is it your wish that I write to Papa at once?"

"No." The monosyllable came out with the force of a pistol shot. "On no account are you to do so. I will not have Thomas believe that I am like to fail him in the duty he has put upon me. He must not be told of my—my slight indisposition."

"But, Aunt Clara . . ."

"Clarissa, must I repeatedly check you of this habit of arguing? If you continue with it, you are likely to find yourself in serious trouble. It comes, of course, from your mother. Her wilfulness must have great distressed Thomas."

With difficulty Crissa prevented herself from retorting that the one person her mother had not argued with was her father. When, on one occasion, Crissa had expressed astonishment at her high-spirited mother's submissive attitude, she had replied, "You may argue with gentlemen friends, even with your betrothed, Crissa. Never with your husband. That you will learn in your own time."

Crissa had tossed her head and declared she would never marry in that case, for no man was going to lord it over her.

Her mother had smiled tolerantly. "You will change your mind, dear child, when you also learn to love."

Aunt Clara's voice brought Crissa back to the present. "I have no intention of dying before I have carried out the service my brother has requested of me."

Tentatively Crissa remarked, "It was Dr. Leland's opinion, ma'am, that our presence here would place too great a strain on you."

The brown eyes flashed. "What right had Dr. Leland to voice such an opinion? This is *my* house. *I* decide who comes and goes. I am prepared to be bled by him and to swallow the potions he prescribes, however unpleasant they may prove. But as to ordering my life to suit his ideas, that I will not do. You may tell him so before he comes to my room this evening. I am not disposed to exert myself arguing with him as well as with you."

"Very well, ma'am. Hetty and I will try not to cause you any more anxiety than we can help. Is there anything I can do for you now that will ease you?"

"You may send your sister to read to me. Her voice is more pleasing than yours since she rarely raises it. And, Clarissa . . ." The girl paused at the door. "I cannot forbid you to speak to Lieutenant de Beauvoir since he is under the same roof. But you will confine your meetings to those which are unavoidable, and any conversation you have with him will be restricted to subjects which are considered proper between a lady and gentleman."

Crissa curbed her impatience. "Lieutenant de Beauvoir finds the evenings rather long and tedious, I believe, after the curfew bell has rung. He has kindly offered to teach me to play chess. I assume that would meet with your approval, ma'am?"

Aunt Clara folded her hands primly together. "I consider that particular pastime to be quite within the bounds of propriety, provided . . ." Her eyes allowed no evasion, "Provided your sister or your maid sits with you, and you leave the door open."

Despite her irritation, Crissa had a desire to giggle. But she kept a straight face as she answered. "Thank you, Aunt Clara. I do assure you that Monsieur de Beauvoir has not given me the slightest reason to believe he would step beyond the bounds of propriety of which you speak."

The old lady regarded her coldly. "I had never supposed he would. The doubt in my mind is entirely on your account."

Crissa was no longer amused. As soon as she joined Hetty she burst out angrily, "Just because I have 'red hair' as they choose to call it; because I speak my mind and openly admit I enjoy the company of young men, everyone seems to regard me as a wanton. It is bad enough to have to endure such remarks from Papa and Aunt Clara. But even her detestable housekeeper and that odious doctor are assured that I shall come to a bad end when, after all, it was you . . ." She broke off and went on her knees beside her sister's chair. "Oh, dearest, I am sorry. Hetty, forgive me, that was cruel."

Sadly the younger girl shook her head. "What you were about to say is true. Except that with me, there was only one young man and there will never be another. That is why, despite all the difficulties, I so long to hold his child in my arms."

"You still feel its movements?"

"Of course. Why do you keep asking that question so anxiously?" Hetty smiled affectionately at her sister. "I declare you are as eager to be an aunt as I am to become a mother."

Crissa sat back on her heels. "I vow I had not realised your child would make me that. It makes me feel quite old and solemn."

Her expression indeed was solemn but she was feeling very young and uncertain as she confronted Dr. Leland that evening. Still smarting under his words and her aunt's attitude, she hoped fervently that he would not provoke her to such anger as she had experienced as a result of his first visit.

"Has there been some change?" he asked. "Is that why you wished to see me before I go upstairs?"

With all the dignity she could muster she preceded him into the drawing-room. It felt damp and chill and she wrapped the yellow paisley shawl she had draped over her white gown more closely about her. She noticed as he stood by her chair that Dr. Leland looked tired; that his boots were caked with mud, his leather breeches stained. His cravat was awry and a waistcoat button missing. His short curly hair, which so contrasted with his strong features, was unruly.

He said, becoming aware of her scrutiny, "I must apologise for my dishevelled appearance, Miss Conway. I was foolish enough to urge my horse too near a bog. He took fright and threw me."

"You were not hurt?" she enquired out of common courtesy.

"Fortunately, no. Merely put out of temper."

That was nothing unusual, she thought, judging from what she had seen of him so far. Then, noting his impatient frown, she told him of Aunt Clara's determination that her brother should not be given the news of her illness and that her nieces should remain at Grimstone.

His frown deepened. Then he shrugged his broad shoulders. "If this is what she wishes, she must have her way, I suppose. In any case, I do not imagine that your visit will last much longer. For your sister will doubtless wish to return home in time to prepare for her confinement."

Crissa stared down at her clasped hands. "The confinement is to be here," she told him in a low voice.

"*Here!*" he exclaimed in astonishment. "In this house? But surely . . ."

Crissa rose to her feet and faced him. She chose her words carefully. "Dr. Leland, when the time comes we shall doubtless be obliged to call upon your services. But I cannot think there is the slightest necessity for you to be made aware of the circumstances leading to my sister and I coming to this house. They are—they are not such as I wish to discuss."

Stiffly he inclined his head. "I beg your pardon, Miss Conway. I had no idea that I was treading upon delicate ground. As you say, my duty at a lying-in is to deliver the child safely, not to enquire into its parenthood."

She clenched her hands. "Sir, it is obvious you misunderstand me. My sister is married—was married, rather, for she is now widowed."

"But she is so young."

"Yes. She is eighteen."

He was silent for a few moments. Then he said, "I apologise for my wrong assumption. When is the child expected?"

"In just over two months."

"Your sister is in good health?"

"At the moment, yes. But she has never been strong."

"Do you wish me to see her?"

Crissa pulled at her shawl, "There is no reason why you should that I am aware of. Phoebe knows exactly what to look for."

"Phoebe?"

"Our maid. You need not look so disapproving. She is the eldest of ten children and therefore has had much experience."

"Was that the girl who . . . ?"

" 'Provoked an ugly scene,' to use your words? Yes, the same. She was, however, acting in what she believed to be my sister's interest. She thought the old crone was ill-wishing Hetty's unborn child, destroying it with a look."

He exclaimed in disgust, "You are not telling me, surely, that you believe such things can happen? In any case, why should old Mother Hawkins wish any harm to your sister's child?"

"Phoebe overheard Martha," Crissa began; then seeing his expression, broke off. "There are reasons why this baby will not be welcomed by—by certain people."

"So a sinister scheme has been thought up to rid your sister of it by what is termed the 'evil eye'? Great heaven! I thought you to be a young woman of intelligence for all you are misguided in some ways."

Her anger flared. Determinedly controlling it, she said icily, "Had you not better go up to your patient now, Dr. Leland? Aunt Clara will doubtless be wondering why our interview has taken so long."

He laughed shortly and gave her a mocking bow. "How kind of you to remind me of my duty, ma'am. Is it your self-appointed mission to put all men in their place? Or do you reserve that pleasure for my benefit alone?"

For the second time he left her standing in the drawing-room, lost for words. As she heard his footsteps ascending the stairs she remembered what Armand had told her: "Paul is not a man who finds it easy to talk to ladies. I do not think he likes them on the whole. There was a young woman . . . a quarrel . . ."

That, she decided, was not to be wondered at in the least. And the young woman, whoever she might be, was well out of the affair. Whereas she and Hetty, and even poor well-meaning Phoebe, were likely to endure a great deal from Paul Leland's tongue in the weeks to come.

"It cannot be allowed, Mademoiselle Clarissa," declared Armand, "that you continue in this restricted life. For your sister, even though she is younger than you, it is different. She is a widow, and in her state . . ." He spread his hands. "But for you, no. You might as well be living in a cloister. The other young ladies of the district—and there is not one as beautiful or charming as you—are finding the company of the French officers much to their liking. We give musical concerts. We divert ourselves and the townspeople with plays. It is unthinkable that you should any longer be deprived of such innocent entertainments."

Indeed the past few weeks had been the most tedious Crissa ever remembered. Each morning, if fine, she and Hetty were permitted a sedate stroll up and down the turnpike road, to provide them with "necessary exercise." They spent the rest of the day helping Martha in the kitchen, sewing in Aunt Clara's room, reading to her. Crissa's one pleasure had been the chess games with Armand, but the opportunities for these seemed rare. All the while she was made fully aware that it was Hetty's company, despite the fact that her sister had arrived under a cloud, that their aunt preferred. From this realisation Crissa drew the hope that Hetty could so win her way into favour that, when the time came, Aunt Clara might listen to her pleas that she be allowed to keep her child. Against that hope Crissa had to set the knowledge that their aunt was devoted to her brother Thomas and was unlikely to flout his will. For the time being, she could only await events and pray that Hetty might continue in ignorance of what was planned.

"I should greatly enjoy some diversion," Crissa said wearily. "As you say, it is all but a nun's existence I am leading."

"I have an idea," Armand told her eagerly. "There is a widow, Mrs. Barlow, who is most kind to us Frenchmen. She often entertains two officers of Hussars of the same age as her sons who are overseas. She is known to Miss Conway and her character is above reproach. She shall chaperone you."

"Do you really think Aunt Clara would consent? In any case, would this lady be willing?"

"I will go at once and ask her." He glanced at his watch, and pulled a face. "You see? I still say, 'I will go' just as if I am not as restricted as you are in a different way. Soon, when the winter months come, we must be in our lodgings by five o'clock, and then . . ." He shrugged expressively.

"It is certainly very early," Crissa sympathised. "Almost they treat you like children."

"Have you not seen the notice posted up in the town?" His voice was mockingly severe as he quoted. " 'And if they stay out later they are liable to be taken up and sent to the Agent for such misconduct.' " He made a tying gesture. " 'Taken up and sent.' Like a package, n'est-ce pas?"

"You accept such conditions very courageously."

He shook his head. "Courage is not needed here, mademoiselle. On the battlefield, or in action at sea, that is where one must show bravery. Here . . ." He spread his hands out in the familiar gesture. "Here is needed patience and the philosophy to make the best of things." Then, frowning, he added, "There are prisoners who need great fortitude, those in the hulks where life is a living hell, or in such places as the depot at Princetown."

"You have spoken of that place before. Is it so very dreadful there?"

"I think it to be like most situations in life. If one is fortunate enough to have money one can survive comfortably enough. But for the others . . ." Ruefully he shook his head.

Crissa recalled the line of prisoners trudging along the highway in the pouring rain the day she and

Hetty had come to Grimstone. Many of them, she had noticed, were without proper clothing or shoes, their bodies looking like scarecrows in their rags.

"It is the same in all the depots," Armand went on seriously, "or in the prison ships, I believe—anywhere that men are herded together in great numbers and utterly degraded. Some will preserve a standard of decency, others will degenerate into animals, scavenging for crusts and cabbage stumps. The worst are the gamblers who stake all they have, clothes, bedding, even their rations, so that . . . Oh, mademoiselle, forgive me. I have distressed you."

She had covered her eyes as if to shut out the picture he painted. Very gently Armand lowered her hands from her face and held them lightly imprisoned.

"Paul is so very wrong in what he says about you. Your heart is warm and full of sympathy. Your sister's refusal to speak to me, or to any other Frenchman, I can understand. But you . . . You do not hate us, do you?"

She was very conscious of the pressure of his fingers, that he was leaning very close to her. "I am not acquainted with any other of your countrymen, Monsieur de Beauvoir. But I would find it impossible to hate you. You have been so very kind to me, when I greatly needed a friend."

He raised her hands to his lips. This time it was not her fingertips he kissed, but the palms. She found it altogether a pleasurable sensation.

"I must go, monsieur," she murmured, but her words lacked conviction. "There are many tasks needing my attention."

He still held her hands and she made no real attempt to free herself. "My name is Armand," he said. "It is not at all difficult to pronounce. Try it."

"*Bon!*" he exclaimed delightedly when she did so. "Yours is much more difficult for me. Clareesa. Creesa."

She laughed up at him. "You cannot gammon me like that. You speak English perfectly when you wish. I declare you put on an accent when it suits you. I think you do it to impress."

"I do it to attract the ladies," he told her. "You find it attractive?"

"I think you are quite vain enough, Armand, without my answering that question. And I dare say that amongst these other young officers you are so anxious for me to meet, I shall find one whose accent is positively irresistible."

His smile was confident. "Possibly. But they will not have my advantages. They do not see you every day, or at your window when you are so charmingly *en négligé.*"

"That is unfair. I was not aware, that first morning, that you were in the garden."

"Not then," he conceded. "But there have been times since when you have passed so casually, so innocently, before your window, and I think you were perfectly aware . . ."

He laughed as she pulled away from him and hurried upstairs. Inside her bedroom she leaned against the door and gave way to her own amusement. This was a game she knew well enough how to play and much enjoyed. If only the good widow would invite her to the entertainments Armand had mentioned. If only Aunt Clara would give her consent.

Mrs. Barlow's letter was carefully worded. Miss Conway, she was sure, could not possibly take exception to her nieces attending so innocent an entertainment as a musical concert given by the French officers whose courteous behaviour was well known. Now that her own daughters were married and far away she would consider it a great privilege to chaperone two such charming young ladies, much as she regretted the indisposition which made it impossible for their aunt to accompany them.

Crissa waited with fingers crossed for Aunt Clara's reaction. To her delighted astonishment, the old lady gave her consent. Hetty, however, was adamant in her refusal.

"You do not suppose I am going to exhibit myself while I look like this?"

"With the present loose style of gown, and if you wear a cloak, it will not be noticed at all," Crissa assured her.

"Of course it will." Hetty turned away, a determined set to her mouth.

"That is not the real reason, is it?" Crissa asked with sudden insight. "You will not go because the music is provided by *French* officers? Can you not forget your bitterness just for this once, Hetty?"

"I never will. But that need not stop you going, dear. It is not fair that you should suffer for my sake." She caught hold of Crissa's hands and squeezed them. "Go and enjoy yourself. And if you *are* falling in love with Monsieur de Beauvoir, I cannot blame you. I believe that women like you and Mama were born to have always some young man at your feet. And I did not think that Harry would satisfy you for long."

Crissa asked anxiously, "Are you suggesting that I am incurably fickle?"

"Of course not. You know full well that Mama had her admirers up to the day she died. That is not to say she was not entirely devoted and loyal to Papa. Some women cannot help attracting men, Crissa. You are one of them."

Crissa studied her sister. "There have been times lately when you made me feel years younger than you. Is it perhaps being *enceinte* which gives you this air of maturity?"

"I have faced so much in so short a space. Perhaps that has aged me beyond my years. But at times I am still very frightened, Crissa. Then I need you, as I always have. You will not desert me, will you?"

Crissa answered gravely, "I failed you once, Hetty, by not taking sufficient care of you, by being so concerned in my own affairs that I did not see what was happening to you. I will not fail you again, I promise you."

Several of the French officers had hired a carriage of sorts to bring their English friends to the concert which was to be held in a barn on the further side of the town. Crissa found herself crowded into this rickety vehicle between Armand and Mrs. Barlow, a dark-haired pretty woman, while opposite sat a young officer resplendent in grey and red, and a bluff farmer and his cheerful wife. It was early evening as they lumbered through the crowded

streets. Not even in Totnes had Crissa seen so
many people; shopkeepers in their best clothes,
farmers on their sturdy Dartmoor ponies, their
wives riding pillion; the dignitaries of the town
dressed soberly in dark tail-coats and tight trousers.
Some wore old-fashioned high hats which made
them look seven feet tall. On all sides Crissa saw
the bright colours of the officers' dress. Some coats,
she noticed, had lost a button or two, or the frog-
ging was torn and frayed, or there were slits which
had been carefully mended. Beside her, Armand
was more handsome than ever in his naval uniform
with the cocked hat. There was a patch on his right
shoulder and she remembered his telling her that
was where he had been wounded. She was very
moved by the sight of these young men who had
dressed up in the gay uniforms in which they must
have been taken prisoner, to attend an entertainment devised for the enjoyment of those they must
consider their enemies. There was nothing warlike
in their bearing this evening. They were laughing
amongst themselves, conversing amicably with the
townspeople, escorting the young women of this
country district with as much gallantry as if they
were promenading in the Bois de Boulogne.

Armand handed Crissa down from the carriage
as if she had been a duchess. She wore a white
low-necked gown with puff sleeves and a band of
green ribbon threaded under the high bosom. There
were tiny bows of the same material at neck and
hem. Her bonnet of golden brown velvet matched
her cloak. She stepped down carefully, drawing her
skirt up a little to show that even her heeless slippers sported a green bow. She saw by Armand's

eyes that he had noticed, that he totally approved of her appearance. She rested her hand on his arm as they walked towards the barn, followed by Mrs. Barlow and the young captain, the farmer and his wife lagging a little behind.

It was just as they were nearing the building that Crissa's garter snapped. She stifled an exclamation of dismay and hoped that Armand had not heard. With every step she could feel her stocking slipping down her leg.

"I think I have left my reticule in the carriage," she said, drawing aside and praying he had not noticed it in her hand, which she now kept hidden beneath her cloak.

"I will go quickly and fetch it," Armand offered at once. "Or the carriage will have gone. You will wait here? I will not be a moment."

Mrs. Barlow, separated from her by the crowd of people entering the barn, had not noticed, Crissa saw thankfully. She looked around her and saw a broken wall jutting out at such an angle that it would effectively hide her. Making sure that no one was looking, she slipped behind it. Hastily she took off her slipper and peeled off the stocking, tucking it into the pocket of her cloak. She was about to emerge from her hiding-place when she heard men's voices on the other side. One of them she recognised at once as Paul Leland's.

He sounded amused as he asked, "And the story of Etienne and the milestone is true?"

His companion was a Frenchman. "*Mais certainement*. Etienne, as you know, is—how you say—botanist? He see a flower that he want, in a place beyond the mile limit. So he pick up the milestone.

*Mon Dieu,* he must be a Samson, for it is made of—of . . ."

"Granite," Dr. Leland supplied.

*"Cest vrai.* And he carry it to where is the plant, pick *la petite fleur* and carry back the milestone to where it belong. So! He has not broken his parole. *Ne seriez-vous pas d'accord?"*

The doctor burst out laughing. It was a pleasant sound. And to Crissa's ears his lighthearted tone was in strange contrast to the coldness to which she was accustomed in his voice.

He said, "It is a point which could be argued in law, doubtless, like the excuse of your Hussar friend who says he cannot be blamed for going beyond bounds when he is fishing, since it is the trout who lead him on and he cannot disappoint the trout."

The other joined in his mirth. "You must admit that life would be intolerable for us without such little escapades."

"I agree." The doctor's voice grew serious. "But, Pierre, I think you must be more careful in future. This new prisoners' agent will not tolerate any laxity. The Transport Board are becoming more vigilant in this district since there have been so many escapes from Launceston."

*"Mais pas ici.* Here we are all gentlemen. We do not break our word of honour."

"Not you, certainly, or Etienne or Armand. But there *are* those amongst you who might try. Most of the townspeople, as you know, are in sympathy with you, and more than one would be perfectly willing to help an escaping officer for a consideration."

Crissa flattened herself against the stones. Any

chance of slipping out of her hiding-place unob-
served had passed. She could see the crown of Paul
Leland's beaver hat, only a foot or two from her.
However anxiously Armand might be searching for
her by now, she could not simply walk out from
behind the wall without an explanation. It would
lead to much speculation and she was not prepared
to give Dr. Leland any more excuses to criticise
her. Besides, they would think she had been eavesdropping, which in fact she was being forced to
do, unless she were to stop up her ears.

"There are some who will give—what is the word
—bribes? And those who will accept them," the
Frenchman agreed. "*Naturellement*, if a man risks
aiding a *fugitif*, he will expect *la grande récom-
pense*. The punishment is to be made more heavy
for that offence, *n'est-ce pas?*"

"Transportation, you mean? That is Lord Castle-
reagh's idea. The new agent here would be in favour of the Bill, I am sure. He does not think fines
or imprisonment severe enough. In any case, there
are such discrepancies. In March of this year a
moorman was fined five pounds and given twelve
months' imprisonment for procuring a disguise for
a prisoner, whereas a man of higher standing . . ."

"Such as yourself?"

There was a moment's silence, while Crissa held
her breath. Then the doctor spoke again, grimly.

"You are not suggesting, I trust, that *I* would be
willing to help Frenchmen to escape?"

"Not officers on parole, *certainement*. But for
those unfortunates at Princetown, you have so great
a—a *sympathie*."

From his tone Crissa could well imagine Paul Leland's expression as he interrupted his companion. "Sympathy I may have, and a desire to help those who are sick or injured. But I would remind you, Pierre, that I am an Englishman and that in fact you and your compatriots are the enemies of my country. I ask you to be good enough not to repeat the suggestion you have just put forward."

"*Je vous demande pardon,* Monsieur Paul." The officer sounded distressed. "I had no intention to give you offence."

"I take none. Come, let us end this speculative conversation and go inside. It is nearly time for them to start, I think."

With relief Crissa heard them move away. Cautiously she peered around the wall. There were only a few stragglers now on the path leading to the barn. And Armand, distractedly searching for her.

Swiftly she joined him. "I am so sorry," she apologised breathlessly. "I—I discovered I had my reticule all the time."

"But where have you been?" he demanded.

The colour rushed into her cheeks and she bent her head so that he could see only the brim of her bonnet.

"Do not ask me to explain, I beg you. It was something I—that no lady ..."

He bent and peered beneath her bonnet. "So?" He gave a little chuckle. "What would your aunt say to such behaviour, Clareesa? Oh, you do not need to tell me. I know exactly what happened. I saw him, making eyes at you as we came along the path."

"Saw—saw him?" she echoed in bewilderment.

"Quite plainly. But you must take care. Monsieur

le Capitaine d'Aubois is not a man to be trusted with young ladies."

She realised with dismay the conclusion he had drawn. She drew herself up and said primly, "You are quite mistaken, Armand. I did not even notice any such gentleman."

As she walked beside him into the barn, she saw that he was puzzled by her behaviour. But she was certainly not prepared to give him any further explanation, no matter what he thought. For if she had, she would have been forced to confess her eavesdropping. Armand and the doctor were close friends. Was it likely he would keep the incident to himself? She would rather by far let Armand retain his suspicion that she had rid herself of him to have a few moments' conversation with another man, than endure further censure from Dr. Leland.

She was scarcely seated before the concert began. The performers, six officers billeted in the town, had borrowed, or fashioned from old lengths of material, eighteenth-century costumes of knee breeches and full-skirted coats with excessively wide cuffs. They wore wigs and lace cravats, and played with great delicacy pieces by Mozart and Haydn with which she was familiar. She leaned forward, absorbed in the music and in watching the performers, greatly enjoying herself. In the pause between two movements she glanced at Armand, who had made it possible for her to come this evening, at Mrs. Barlow who had been kind enough to act as chaperone to an unknown girl. She looked at the townspeople in their best clothes, at the farmers in their homespun breeches and jackets, mingling so amicably with the uniformed men of Napoleon's forces.

Tears came into her eyes. Armand's hand closed over hers. She smiled at him, returning very slightly the pressure of his fingers.

Then, for the first time, she saw that Paul Leland was sitting further along the same row of benches. His eyes were on her, as they had been in church. But now there was a puzzled look in them. He inclined his head towards her, then returned his attention to the stage. Beyond him again, sitting a little apart, was a tall, thin man in dark clothes who instantly reminded Crissa of her father. He had the same humourless eyes, and his pale lips were pressed tightly together.

"Who is that man?" she whispered to Armand in an interval.

He looked where she indicated, and pulled a face. "Mr. Creber, the agent responsible for parole officers. He is not at all popular. The last agent was given to—how do you say?—winking an eye at little harmless escapades some of us indulged in. But this one . . ." He drew down the corners of his mouth. "He has told us he will allow no breaking of the rules at all. At the milestone we must halt and turn about. When the bell rings we must have one foot already inside our lodgings. For those who are foolish enough to try to forge documents, or cheat a shopkeeper . . ." He made an exaggerated gesture of cutting his throat. Then, seeing her dismay, he added quickly, "I was only joking, Crissa. But for any little misdemeanour we will be punished more heavily than before."

"And if any should—should try to escape?"

He frowned. "I would like to be able to tell you that would never happen, that no officer who has given his word would break it. It is not so, unfortunately. For that crime the punishment is clearly laid down by the Transport Board who make all the rules. Such men would be sent to prison at once —that is, if they were caught."

The music started up again, the violins very sweet, the cello melodious. Crissa was only half listening now. She was remembering something Armand had said when Paul Leland had come upon them sitting together on the bench beside the river.

"Paul is so good to all of us prisoners of war. He even goes to the depot at Princetown . . . It is said that when a prisoner escapes, Paul's house should be the first to be searched."

Dr. Leland had been angry, as he had been angry this evening when the unseen Frenchman had made a similar suggestion. Armand had asserted he had been joking and the officer called Pierre, upon the doctor's display of annoyance, had immediately apologised. But the thought had evidently been in their minds, and it was one which did not please Paul Leland.

Crissa glanced again at the agent and saw that his attention was not on the performance. Instead, he was looking searchingly, and with an expression which again reminded Crissa of her father, at the doctor and the animated faces of the French officers in whose midst he sat.

She could not have said what caused her to shiver. Certainly it was not cold in the barn which was packed so closely with human beings. Nor was there the slightest draught to be detected. "Somebody walking on your grave," Phoebe would have said, and Paul Leland would have been the first to chide her for her fancies.

Mrs. Barlow insisted on accompanying Crissa back to Grimstone House and on reporting to Aunt Clara. The old lady, for her part, instructed that Mrs. Barlow should be given refreshment in the drawing-room where Martha had lit the fire in readiness for their return. She would tolerate no excuses on the part of her younger niece for not joining the little party, so Hetty had perforce at last to sit in the same room as Armand.

With the greatest delicacy he stood at a little distance from her, engaging Crissa in an animated conversation about the concert, leaving the younger girl to talk to Mrs. Barlow. Just once Hetty's eyes met the Frenchman's. Briefly he smiled at her and inclined his head in a formal gesture. The smile she forced in return was stiff-lipped, without warmth, and she turned immediately back to their visitor. Armand glanced at Crissa, lightly shrugging his shoulders, but his eyes reflected the regret she felt in her own heart that her sister's bitterness should be directed even towards him.

Martha had already retired to bed, so Phoebe waited upon them, well pleased that her young ladies should have some company at last. When eventually Mrs. Barlow rose to take her leave, Armand's face was troubled.

"I would so like to escort you home, madame. But as you know . . ."

"It is two hours past your curfew time," the widow finished for him. "The concert ended later than expected. It is as well that Mr. Creber, the agent, was present or there might have been questions asked."

Armand and Crissa went with her to the door. "If it were merely a question of breaking a rule for which one might be punished, I would most willingly accompany you," the young man assured her earnestly. "But when one has given one's word of honour . . ."

Mrs. Barlow laid a hand on his arm. "I assure you, Armand, you have no need to explain. I understand the position perfectly."

"May I not come with you, ma'am?" Crissa suggested. "It is not right that you should walk home alone."

"My dear child, it is scarcely any distance, and a bright night. I assure you I shall come to no harm, though it was a kind thought on your part." Her smile was quite youthful. "And if you escorted me, who then would bring *you* home? We should spend all night going to and fro."

Armand laughed. "*C'est vrai.* We will both escort you to the gate, however. That at least can be called within bounds, surely?"

The moon was bright as they parted at the end of the drive. Armand drew Crissa's arm through his as they walked back. "Now tell me truthfully, did you find an excuse to get rid of me so that you could meet le Capitaine d'Aubois? If so, I shall not only be jealous but concerned. I know that you are not without experience of men, but I cannot think you have ever met one such as he."

He was no longer smiling but looking down at her with a gravity which made him seem a good deal older. She saw that the concern he spoke of was quite genuine, that he was truly worried on her account.

She returned his look without evasion. "Armand, I ask you to believe that I would not even know this gentleman if I saw him. The reason for pretending I had left my reticule was—was quite different."

"And you do not wish to tell me?"

"I . . ." She could no longer meet his eyes. "Will you accept the explanation that it was something to do with my—my attire, which necessitated my finding a place to be out of sight, just for a minute or two? And then, two gentlemen stopped on the other side of the wall where I was hidden and I could not emerge until they had gone. For if I had done so . . ." She came to a halt, glancing anxiously up to see if he believed her.

With relief she saw that he was smiling, his eyes bright with amusement. "Was that it?" he asked, laughing. "Such things I understand. They happen to my sisters also. Poor Crissa. I would have stood guard if you had told me."

She said with dignity, "It is not usual, sir, to discuss such matters with a gentleman."

"*Oh, mais vous êtes trop modeste.* I should beg your pardon, perhaps, for forcing you into an explanation which has made you blush." He put two fingers under her chin and tilted up her face. "You are the most delightful mixture, Clareesa, of gaiety and seriousness, of rebelliousness and sudden primness. Your visit here does not please you, I know. But *I* am glad you came." He bent his head and kissed her lightly on the cheek. "Ah no, do not scold me," he said quickly as she drew away. "There is too much scolding in this house. Besides"—his eyes teased her again—"I do not think you would really mean it. It was not so very distasteful, was it?"

She put a hand to her cheek. "No," she whispered. "I did not find it distasteful in the least."

He kissed her again, on the lips this time. She made no resistance but put up her hand and stroked his hair. His arms went about her, but before he could repeat the kiss she drew away.

"If you please, Armand, that is enough. It was most kind of you to invite me this evening. I have enjoyed myself so very much."

And this interlude not the least, she admitted to herself as she started towards the house. Armand slipped his arm lightly about her waist.

"You are very sweet, Crissa. I think I fall in love with you. What would your Aunt Clara say to that?"

Crissa sighed. "I do not believe she would understand what you meant. For one cannot suppose that she has ever done such a thing in her life."

"But you have, Crissa. Many times?"

"Several times. Not seriously."

"And now?" As they reached the door he turned her to face him.

"I don't know, Armand. I like you very much indeed."

"But I am French, *hein?* Although you do not share your sister's bitterness, I am still an enemy of your country."

She put a hand on his arm. "No, Armand, that would make no difference. One does not guide one's heart in that way. But—it is difficult to explain.

I feel uncertain of myself at present. Perhaps it is because I am so worried over Hetty."

His fingers closed over hers. "Poor little Crissa. I understand. I will not worry you. But remember that I am here, willing to serve you in any way I can. And if one day you find you can love me . . ."

"I think it very possible," she said softly.

As they entered the house, Hetty was starting up the stairs. She turned at Crissa's greeting. Her shawl slipped from her shoulders. Immediately Armand ran forward to retrieve it for her. With a startled exclamation she shrank back, catching her heel in the fringes of the shawl. She clutched desperately at the banister, but missed. Armand stretched out his arms. But he was off balance. Her weight bore him backwards. There was a mingling of grey and lavender and navy blue as they fell together down the bottom six stairs.

Crissa closed her eyes, pressed her hands to her mouth to stop herself screaming. When she looked again, Hetty was lying where she had fallen, quite still. Armand was easing his arm from beneath her. His right arm, Crissa noticed even in that dreadful moment, and he was wincing with pain. He raised stricken eyes to Crissa as she went on her knees beside him.

"*Mon Dieu! Quelle catastrophe!* What have I done?"

Crissa bent over her sister, chafing her hands. "Hetty. Hetty."

The younger girl opened her eyes. They had a dull uncomprehending look. "Will it be—the end?" she asked brokenly. "Will I—lose—my baby?"

"Of course not," Crissa answered with more conviction than she felt. "I will fetch Phoebe. She will know what to do. Do not try to move, dearest."

Armand was still kneeling there, holding Hetty's hand, when Crissa returned with Phoebe. The maid's eyes were wide with dismay, but swiftly she controlled her anxiety and said in a voice which calmed them all, "Will you be good enough to carry Miss Henrietta up to her bed, sir? That's the best place for her, whatever happens."

To Crissa's relief, Hetty made no attempt to resist as Armand raised her gently and carried her upstairs and along the landing to the bedroom. As they neared Aunt Clara's door, she called out to know what had happened. For a moment they stood in silence, not knowing how to reply. Then Armand called cheerfully, "It is nothing, Miss Conway. I slipped down some stairs, that is all. I am so sorry to have disturbed you."

In the candlelit bedroom he laid Hetty on the big feather bed. Again, one part of Crissa's mind registered that he was in pain. Probably the fall had jarred his wound.

"What is likely to happen?" she asked Phoebe in a whisper. "Will the fall have . . . ?" She could not voice her fear.

Phoebe's face was troubled. "There's no knowing yet, Miss Clarissa. But I think it's most likely. After all, she's only six weeks off her time."

"Then what are we to do?" Crissa scarcely recognised her own voice.

Armand straightened. His eyes still showed shocked dismay. But his face was set, his voice firm. "There is only one thing to do. To get Dr. Paul here as soon as possible. I will go at once and fetch him."

"Oh yes!" Crissa exclaimed thankfully. "Oh yes, Armand, please. And hurry, I beg you, hurry."

She was aware, as she tried to soothe Hetty, now trembling violently and in tears, of his running footsteps down the drive, of the distant clang of the gate. Then there was only the sound of her sister's sobbing. And the room was suddenly very cold, and fear was in every flickering shadow.

5

At the first sound of hooves in the drive Crissa snatched up a candle and went swiftly downstairs. Paul Leland seemed borne into the house on a shaft of moonlight. He flung his riding coat across a settle, his hat and whip on top.

"What has happened?" he asked, striding across the hall with his saddle-bag slung over his arm.

Crissa had too much difficulty in keeping up with him as he took the stairs two at a time, to reply at once. But as he turned into the passage leading to the back of the house, she caught at his arm.

"Not that way. This door."

He raised his eyebrows. "Miss Conway has changed her bedroom?"

"It is not my aunt who needs you," she said in surprise. "Surely Armand explained?"

There was a shuttered look on his face. "Not very

clearly," he answered as if feeling his way. "If not your aunt, who is it you called me to attend?"

"My sister. Oh, I thought Armand would have told you what happened," she said impatiently. "She had a fall, at the bottom of the stairs. She— she does not seem to be in pain at the moment but she is very frightened that the baby . . ."

"How long?" he demanded.

"I—I do not know," she answered dully. "It seems hours ago."

"I mean, how far advanced is her pregnancy?" he said with forced patience.

"Seven and a half months. Dr. Leland . . ." Impulsively she put a hand on his arm. "Is it—very dangerous?"

His face was impassive. "I cannot say without seeing her. It depends on a number of things. From the little I have seen of your sister, I should not judge her very robust."

"That is true. She tires easily and . . . Oh, please. *Please* help her."

His hand on the door knob, he turned and gave her a searching look. "That, I assume, is what you called me for."

Following him into the room, Crissa felt a bitter resentment that it was this man who, she was sure, now held Hetty's life in his hands. If only they were at home, with white-haired Dr. Poultenay who had delivered both herself and Hetty and who would be gentle and soothing and not speak in this brusque, unfriendly tone.

In the next ten minutes, however, she received one of the greatest surprises of her life and witnessed such a change in a man as she would not have credited without the evidence of her own eyes and ears.

Hetty shrank against the pillows at sight of him. "Not you," she whispered. "I do not want you!"

Deliberately he put his saddle-bag on the floor and sat down in the chair Crissa had vacated. Over his shoulder he gave a warning glance at Phoebe, hovering protectively.

"Now, Mrs. . . ."

"Stanhope," Crissa supplied when Hetty did not help him.

"Thank you. Mrs. Stanhope, I fully realise that you can have no happy remembrance of our first meeting. But that is past and forgotten. You are no longer an imperious young lady in a carriage which is blocking my passage. You are instead someone who is in need of my help. And I am here to give it."

As he spoke, his fingers were resting gently on her wrist. Crissa thought Hetty could scarcely be even aware that he was feeling her pulse. His voice was quiet and calm, his face relaxed though his eyes, she realised, were taking in every detail of her sister's appearance.

"Now," he said, turning back the bedclothes. "Are you willing for me to examine you?"

Hetty cast an appealing glance at her sister. Crissa moved to the bedside and Hetty said in a childlike voice which caught at Crissa's heart, "Yes. Yes, if it is necessary to save my baby."

When he had done, Paul straightened and smiled down at the frightened girl. "You must prepare yourself, Mrs. Stanhope, for the child to be born somewhat earlier than expected. He will be with you tonight, possibly, or tomorrow morning."

Hetty gasped and clung to Crissa's hand. "Alive? Will he live?"

The doctor's smile was as gentle and comforting as a woman's, "Why should he not? You have given him, and yourself, a jolt, and I dare say he would prefer to stay where he is. But that, I fear, is not possible. So we must make his entry into the world as easy as we can, must we not? And that needs your help as well as mine." He moved to the door. "I am going to fetch my other saddle-bag which has things in it I may need. Miss Conway will perhaps be kind enough . . ."

Crissa, taking the hint, followed him from the room.

"Where can I talk to you?" he asked quietly.

"In the drawing-room. The fire is probably alight there." Crissa glanced along the passage. "Aunt Clara must be sleeping very heavily."

"The potion I prescribed would be responsible for that."

In the drawing-room she faced him, waiting in silence for what he would say. He held out his hands to the dying fire; broad hands with rather thick fingers. More like a farmer's, Crissa thought. Yet she had just seen how flexible and gentle they could be.

"I assume you wish me to speak quite openly to you, Miss Conway? Since you have no mother or any married relative here . . ."

"This is no time to be concerned with what is or is not considered proper. Please tell me the truth,

Dr. Leland. It is only Hetty who needs to be buoyed up with hope even if there is none."

"I would not say there is no hope. But there *is* danger, as I think you are well aware, to both your sister and the child. May I ask you a question?"

For a moment her former antipathy returned. "You have not failed to speak exactly as you wished on previous occasions. Why ask permission now?"

He ignored her jibe. "You mentioned to me that this child would be unwelcome to certain people. But not to your sister, apparently?"

"Oh, no. Hetty desperately wants this baby. Her husband, as I told you, is dead. She loved him very dearly. The thought of the child is all she lives for at present."

"I see." He stood frowning down at the fire. "That makes it more difficult. For it may be necessary for me to make a decision whether to . . ." He glanced at her. She swallowed hard and finished for him.

"To sacrifice the child? If it comes to that, then . . ." She turned away, her eyes filling with tears, and bit hard on her knuckles.

She felt his hand beneath her elbow. His voice was very quiet. "Miss Conway, I am afraid you have no option but to trust me to do what I think best for your sister. You are naturally very distressed. But I would ask you to call on the courage which I think you undoubtedly possess, and to forget your own fears and give your sister all the help you can."

"You wish me to—to stay with her?" she asked in a dismayed whisper.

"I think it would comfort her if you did. Even if we were to send for Mrs. Barlow . . ."

"No. You are right, of course. It is myself she will

**111**

want. Why, only yesterday I promised not to fail her when she needed me. I little thought in what way I would be called upon to keep that promise."

Her voice was uncertain and her hands were trembling. The doctor's fingers dug into the flesh of her arm. His tone had altered.

"You will do exactly as I tell you. And you will not, whatever happens, betray your fears to your sister."

She turned to him. His eyes had almost a hypnotic effect upon her, as if through them he were transmitting strength. She nodded without speaking. He released her arm and went swiftly from the room to fetch the instruments which Crissa prayed fervently he would not need to use.

There had never in all her life been so long a night, she was sure. Nor one in which she had need to call upon every ounce of courage she possessed. There were times when she thought her fingers must crack under the frantic grip of her sister's; when she was sure that not even the muffling bedclothes could keep Hetty's cries from Aunt Clara's ears. She was helped by two things. Not for one moment did Paul's face or voice betray the slighest anxiety or suggestion that all would not go well with both Hetty and the child. And Phoebe, to whom this experience was by no means new, was cheerfully encouraging the whole time.

It was in the early hours of the morning when the doctor rose to his feet. "If you will stand aside now, Miss Conway," he said quietly. "Phoebe, your assistance, please."

Crissa freed herself from Hetty's clinging fingers and moved over to the window. She stood with her back to the room, her hands clasped together, her whole being concentrated in a desperate, silent prayer. A faint light was spreading across the moor. A breeze stirred the leaves in the garden below. From across the valley sounded the deep croak of a raven.

Phoebe exclaimed in alarm, "Don't 'ee do that! 'Tis a bird of ill omen, a raven. 'Twill mean . . ."

"Be quite, girl," the doctor ordered. "Now . . ."

There was a cry from Hetty, then silence. Crissa heard the doctor's heavy breathing, a kind of whimpering sound from Phoebe.

" 'T'aint a mite o' gude, zur. I told 'ee that owd raven's to blame."

Crissa, despite her resolution not to look, turned round. Paul was holding up a little wrinkled creature by its heels, slapping it hard. His face was flushed, his brows drawn fiercely together.

Crissa's control broke. She rushed foward, her hands outstretched. "Don't do that. You'll kill it. You *mean* to kill it."

His hand thrust out to stop her hit her full upon the breast. Mingled with her own cry of pain was another, feeble, protesting.

"Thank God!" Paul exclaimed. "Here, take him. Keep him warm."

Swiftly he wrapped the baby in the shawl Phoebe held out, and thrust it at Crissa. She stood, completely dazed, not even looking at the bundle in her arms.

The doctor's voice was brusque. "Do as I say, Miss Conway. Take him somewhere warm while this girl and I deal with your sister."

She went from the room like someone sleep-walking. In the drawing-room the fire had gone out. She stood in the hall, unable to think clearly. Then she remembered that the kitchen range was never let out. She poked it into life, and drawing up Martha's old rocking chair, sat down. The shutters were closed and the only light was from the glowing coals. The baby whimpered a little, and then was silent.

So he really lived. Hetty's son. Her nephew. A few minutes ago he had been no more than a mystery, a secret hidden within her sister's body. Now he was here, in her arms, a human being despite his tiny size, his fragility. She wanted to hug him tightly to her. Yet he was too small, too new for that.

She rocked to and fro in the firelight, hearing the mice in the wainscot, the odd creaks of an old house, the faint call of the raven in the wood.

Suddenly at that sound, she was afraid again. The child was safe. But Hetty? With what remained of her self-control she forced herself to wait, to obey Paul's instructions and not to rush upstairs to find out what was happening to Hetty.

It seemed a very long time before Paul came to her. He did not speak, but stood beside her chair, looking down at her. In the firelight his face appeared lined and weary. His hair was ruffled and there was blood upon his shirt. In his eyes was an expression she found difficult to interpret—a kind of wondering, lost look as if his own confidence had suddenly deserted him and he was uncertain of himself.

With a visible effort he pulled himself together. His voice was as firm as usual. "Your sister is very tired."

"But she is all right? She will not die?"

"There is still some risk. But I think the fact that her baby is safely born will help her to recover. She is anxious to have him with her now. Some hot bricks, well covered . . ."

"Yes, of course," she said, rising. "Phoebe will see to that."

"She is a sensible girl, your maid, despite her ridiculous superstitions. She was of considerable help to me."

"I am glad. She is devoted to Hetty."

She realised that they were making polite, stilted conversation. She said humbly, "Dr. Leland, I owe you an apology. I behaved very foolishly just now. I am sorry."

There was sympathy in his voice. "It was understandable. The first time I saw so small a creature forced so fiercely into life I too was startled. In fact, Miss Conway, I have nothing but the greatest admiration for your conduct during this crisis."

A spark of her former antagonism made her reply tartly, "That is indeed a change of attitude." But as she went with him towards the door, she felt ashamed of such a remark. She turned to him and said earnestly, "From my heart I thank you for what you have done tonight. I—I was so afraid. And so was Hetty. But when you came. It was like . . ." She found it difficult to express what she felt. She tried again. "You were so different. I had not imagined that you could be so—so gentle and understanding."

"Perhaps we have both seen each other in a different light during these last few hours. It happens in crises, you know, that people break down the barriers they have erected for—for some reason or another."

"You mean—that is what *I* have done?"

He smiled. "You have, I think you will not deny, shown a side of yourself of which I was previously unaware. I have misjudged you, I fear. I thought you hard, superficial, desiring above all else to be flattered and spoiled. For that, I beg your pardon."

He glanced at the child in her arms. "It is time you took your nephew to his mother, Aunt Clarissa," he said in a tone which was almost teasing.

"That makes me sound so very old, like Aunt Clara. Oh, dear, what *will* she say to all this?"

"I was wondering when that thought would occur to you. I must go home now, but will return within a few hours. If you wish, I will break the news to her then."

"It is very kind of you to offer. But I think . . . You see, there are certain circumstances which even yet you are not acquainted with."

"As you wish. But try to sleep a little. You are more exhausted than you realise."

She managed a smile. "That is of little consequence now that Hetty and the child are safe. They will be, won't they, Dr. Leland?"

"I hope so. Truly I think so."

Having settled the baby beside a tired but smiling Hetty, Crissa went to the door with Paul. She was watching him strap on his saddle-bags when she suddenly thought of Armand.

"Where can he be?" she asked. "I do not remember hearing him come back. But surely he would not just have gone to bed. He was anxious about Hetty."

Paul's hand paused on a buckle. "Miss Conway, I think it best I tell you about Armand when I return."

"Why?" Seeing his expression, she demanded urgently, "Why do you look like that? You cannot leave me in suspense. Where *is* Armand?"

"I do not know for certain, but I can guess. Because, of course, in coming for me, Armand broke his parole."

"Oh, I had forgotten that rule!" she exclaimed in dismay. "And he himself, I am sure, never gave it a second thought. For he did not hesitate a moment before going for you. But, surely, no one could hold that against him in such an emergency?"

"If that had been all, certainly neither the local agent nor the Transport Board would have pressed a case against him in these circumstances. But . . ." he hesitated. "Miss Conway, I think you should rest now. You have suffered enough anxiety for the present."

"That means you are withholding bad news. I beg you, tell me at once what has happened. Suspense would be worse than knowing."

He fastened the strap and turned to her. "Very well," he said resignedly. "I was eating a late supper when I heard shouting outside my house and my name called. I went to the door and saw a group of men struggling in the road. In the moonlight I was able to recognise several of them. One was a French officer who has been under suspicion of trying to contact escape agents. Three were local men who had already received rewards for reporting prisoners breaking their parole rules. The other was Armand."

"But what was he doing with them? He went only to fetch you, that I would swear."

"*I* do not question that fact for a moment. But there are those who will, I fear."

She was silent, trying to grasp the implications of what he had told her. Then she asked, "Did you not try to help him? There was a struggle, you said."

"I think Armand's only thought was to try and reach my house. When I got to them, he was on the ground, calling my name. I ordered the men to release him but they would not do so. I tried to pull them away. But Armand shouted at me, 'Go to Grimstone. For pity's sake, go to Grimstone, that is where you are needed.' I did not want to leave him there, but he insisted he could fend for himself. He sounded desperate. 'In God's name, go, or she will die,' he said. And so I came. You will understand now why I thought it was your aunt I had been called to."

In the morning light his face looked grey. She supposed her own had the same drawn look. Involuntarily she shivered.

"You will get chilled here," he said gently. "When I return I hope to have further news, and good news. No real harm can come to him, I am sure, since we both know him innocent of anything but good intentions."

"He was injured," Crissa said dully. "When he fell he hurt the shoulder where he had been wounded, though he tried to hide it." She buried her face in her hands. Her voice was muffled. "It was really Hetty's fault that she fell, not Armand's. He was only trying to retrieve her shawl for her and she drew back. She cannot bear him near her because he is a Frenchman. Yet he went to fetch help for her, without a thought for himself. And she would not even speak to him. How could anything as cruel as this have happened?"

She felt his hands on her shoulders, gentle but firm. "Do not let your courage desert you now. Armand will soon be free again, I am sure. But you must not expect to see him back at once."

She brushed away her tears and raised her head. "How kind you are. The misjudging has not been only on your side."

"Do not be too sure of that. You have seen me these last hours as a doctor. As a man, I am not nearly so—understanding."

Aunt Clara said, "Do you mean to tell me that all this has occurred during the night and I was not roused?"

"We thought it best to let you sleep, ma'am," Crissa explained wearily.

"*We?*"

"Dr. Leland and I. Martha, of course, was already in bed."

The old lady sat erect against her pillows. "You have the effrontery to stand there, as brazen as can be, and inform me that you were present at a confinement conducted by a man young enough to be . . ." Her voice trailed away.

"I pray you, do not upset yourself," Crissa warned in alarm. "I do assure you, ma'am, there was no other course."

"Clarissa, I am astounded at your behaviour."

"May I ask what you would have had me do?"

Crissa burst out. "Dr. Leland told me he had given you a potion to help you to sleep. If you had been roused suddenly, to face such a shock as I myself received, it would, I am sure, have done you great harm."

Aunt Clara pursed her lips, but seemed to accept the point. Crissa pressed her advantage. "Nothing can be altered, Aunt Clara, however much you disapprove of what has happened. Hetty's baby is born. That, surely, is the most important concern to any of us."

"Bring it to me."

Crissa stared at her. The old woman thrust up her chin.

"Are you deaf, girl? Bring the child to me."

Crissa passed her tongue over her lips. "For what purpose?"

"Have you lost your wits? What purpose do you suppose I have save to see for myself that you are speaking the truth?"

Reluctantly Crissa went to fetch the baby. Hetty murmured a weak protest as Crissa took him from her encircling arm.

"It is all right, dearest. Aunt Clara wants to see your son. I will bring him back to you directly."

In her aunt's room she stood some distance from the bed. Impatiently Aunt Clara tapped her fingers on the bedclothes. "Bring it closer. Do you think I am going to bite it?"

Cautiously Crissa approached. She could not rid herself of the suspicion that the old lady wished to harm the child. She knew her fancy to be almost as wild as Phoebe's, but she was filled with anxiety over Armand and near to exhaustion. She kept firm hold of the baby and watched her aunt's every movement.

The thin, wrinkled fingers pulled back the shawl. The old woman's features were expressionless as she looked at the puckered face.

"A boy, you said?"

"Yes."

"And perfect?"

"Yes, quite perfect, save that he is very small."

"Naturally, since he had the misfortune to be premature. Has a wet nurse been arranged for?"

"Not yet. We—we have scarce had time."

"I am surprised, Clarissa. You and Dr. Leland are so in the habit of arranging matters between you. Amongst his patients there must be some woman with more milk than she needs for her own child. So puny a baby will need good nourishment."

"Then you . . . ?" Crissa began, and only just stopped herself from saying, "Then you *wish* him to live?"

Her aunt settled back against the pillows. "Really, Clarissa, I find your conduct extraordinary. For a young woman who is usually far too sure of herself, you are behaving very strangely. One would suppose you to be frightened of me, which, judging from your previous attitude, I cannot believe to be the case."

"I have had no sleep and it has all been very distressing."

The old woman pinched in her nostrils. "I did not think you would admit to weakness, Clarissa. I am disappointed in you." She stopped Crissa's protest with an imperious lift of her hand. "You must be well aware that I do not like you any more than you do me. But, hard as I find it to deal with your rebellious nature, your determination to have your own way is at least something I can recognise. I find this change in you disconcerting. Now leave me, and send Dr. Leland to me the moment he comes."

If her aunt found Crissa's behaviour puzzling, she herself was also at a loss to understand the old lady's attitude. If Aunt Clara knew she had to be rid of the child, why be anxious about its care? Puny as the baby was, it would be so easy to let him die and then Thomas Conway's wishes would be fulfilled. At the thought of her father, Crissa's heart sank. For would she not now be obliged to write to him with the news, and would that not bring the day nearer when Hetty's heart would come near to breaking point?

As she laid the child again beside his mother, and saw the dull eyes light up, the tired smile which yet held pride, Crissa resolved again to find some way for Hetty to keep the baby. But not now. She could plan nothing now, scarcely even think coherently. She was too tired, much too tired.

She lay down, fully dressed, upon the leather sofa in her aunt's little parlour where Phoebe, despite Martha's grumbling, had set a light to the fire. The maid, still cheerful, covered Crissa with a rug.

"Now don't 'ee fret, ma'am, I'll stay with Miss Hetty. And as for the French gentleman, there's nothing you can do until the doctor comes again." She arranged a cushion under Crissa's head. "My, but he was proper clever last night. I never thought he'd save the little mite, I don't mind telling you."

Crissa said sleepily, "I haven't thanked you for

your help, Phoebe. It was a great blessing that Papa allowed you to come here with us."

She did not know how long she slept, but she woke to find Paul standing beside the sofa, looking down at her. Hastily she made to rise, but he pressed her gently back and pulled up a chair.

"It is good that you have had some rest."

The tone of his voice seemed to hold a warning. She still felt sleepy and her tired mind rejected the idea of any more anxiety. She made an attempt to tidy her hair while she played for time.

"Have you seen my sister?"

"Yes. She is naturally very tired, but otherwise well enough."

"And the child?"

"I took the liberty of arranging for a wet nurse to come later in the day. Your sister will not manage, I think, for three or four days after so great a shock."

"Thank you, that was kind. You have also visited Aunt Clara?"

He nodded. "I suspect that despite all my instructions she will not keep to her bed today. You have doubtless learned that Miss Conway likes to keep tight control upon her household?"

"Oh, yes. I learned that very early in my stay here."

She wanted to enlarge upon that, to talk of Hetty and the child, or of anything that would give her an excuse for delaying the news she was sure he was waiting to give her.

She asked at last, "Armand?"

Paul leaned forward, frowning, clasped hands between his knees. "I think you have guessed my report is not good. Believe me, it grieves me to have to tell you what I fear will greatly distress you.

Apart from the gratitude which you naturally feel for his action last night, I believe I am right in thinking you have formed a certain regard for Armand?"

She bent her head. "His company has been most agreeable and he is exceedingly kind."

"Yet I was under the impression that in your opinion all Frenchman should be hated and despised."

"In that you were wrong. It is Hetty who takes such a view and in the circumstances there is some justification for it. I think you are still not aware that her husband, to whom she was married for so short a time, was a naval officer killed while pursuing a French privateer."

"No, I was not aware of that. In that case it is scarcely to be wondered at that she is so resentful. To be widowed so young, with a child on the way . . . That was a cruel blow. I am sorry, Miss Conway. It seems I have been guilty of too hasty a judgment of both you and your sister. Does Mrs. Stanhope know that Armand has not returned?"

"I considered it best to keep that fact from her."

"You were wise. For after the sacrifice Armand made for her last night, I would suspect her attitude may change. To tell you the truth, I found it difficult to reconcile her behaviour on the first day we met with what I saw later of her general appearance and bearing. Had I not had that unfortunat encounter with you on the Plymouth road, I would have judged her as a gentle, sweet-natured young woman."

"That is what she is," Crissa confirmed earnestly. "Which is why I have made every excuse for her attitude."

He stood up and laid an arm along the mantel-shelf. "You are, I think, very devoted to her?"

"I love her more than anyone in the world."

He pushed at a log with his boot. "Even more than Armand?"

For a few moments she regarded him in silence. Then she answered quietly, "I think you are testing me, Dr. Leland. However distressing the news of Armand may prove, I would prefer to have it without further delay."

She pushed down the rug and swung her feet to the ground. The action revealed her ankles in the pale-coloured stockings, and her gay red slippers. Hastily she smoothed the creases from her gown. But Paul was not even looking at her.

He sighed deeply and his voice was heavy with regret. "It is as I suspected. The French officer who was apprehended last night, Captain d'Aubois, was certainly attempting an escape. He had forged documents, money, maps of the district. Two men well known as escape agents and smugglers were discovered waiting with two horses and clothes for disguise, in a wood on the Plymouth road, the same road on which my house stands. It was assumed, when Armand was found heading in that direction late at night, that he was joining his compatriot."

"But his presence there could easily be explained. And since this officer was obviously not the only one trying to escape, have they not caught the second one?"

Gravely Paul shook his head. "No, Miss Conway. Nor are they looking for him."

"I do not understand."

He glanced down at her and again shifted a log a few inches. "They are not looking for a second officer because they are convinced Armand is their man. You see, Captain d'Aubois named him as such!"

She cried out in dismay. "But that could not be." Something stirred in her memory that seemed important. "Armand did not even like this man," she recalled. "He even warned me to have nothing to do with him."

"Were you proposing to associate with him?" Paul asked, his dark brows raised.

"No. It was a misunderstanding. Oh, please do not ask me to explain that now. It is too long a story. I have never even met Captain d'Aubois, but Armand twice spoke of him in terms of the greatest dislike." She suddenly saw the implication of her words. "That perhaps would account for his naming Armand—to settle some private feud."

"You may be right. That, I imagine, will be for a court to discover."

"A court? Do you mean that Armand will be tried on this false charge? Oh, surely, if you go to the agent and explain—or I will write to him telling him the true facts—surely, in that case, Armand will be allowed at once to leave whatever house he is held in?"

He raised his head and looked straight at her. "Armand is not held in a house, Miss Conway. He has been taken to the depot for prisoners at Princetown."

"*Oh, no!*"

Everything that Armand had told her of that

dreadful place rushed into her mind, all the horrible details of hardship and degradation.

"But it is so wrong, so wicked," she protested. "To treat an innocent man thus. The whole affair is a terrible mistake, as anyone who knows Armand must realise. There can hardly have been a French officer in the whole country more strict about keeping his parole, and as for escaping . . ." She rose and clutched at the doctor's arm. "This matter must be cleared up straight away. You must go to Princetown and . . ."

"Certainly I will go, this very day. But you must realise that *my* evidence may not be well received."

"Why not?" she asked in astonishment. "You are a physician, a man respected in the district."

"I am also well known to have the greatest sympathy towards these unfortunate men. I have entertained many of the officers at my house and sometimes taken their part in an argument with a dishonest tradesman. You yourself heard Armand's suggestion that my house should be the first to be searched when an escape has taken place. He said it in jest, but there are those who would . . ."

She did not hear the rest of his sentence. She was remembering a conversation she had not been meant to listen to, between the doctor and a Frenchman called Pierre, and the same idea had been in that officer's mind also.

"Is there any ground for these suspicions?" she wanted to ask outright. Had he in fact harboured an escaped prisoner? But she dared not ask. Instead she said, "Then what is to be done?" Almost as soon as she had spoken, she provided the answer. "I have it. Aunt Clara shall vouch for Armand."

He frowned and shook his head. "I am sorry, but only if all else fails would I venture to ask Miss Conway to do that. The occurrences of last night are sufficiently upsetting for her heart condition without adding this extra worry."

"But she surely must know that Armand is not in the house?"

"I have merely told her that he was taken to the agent for breaking his parole, but that the matter will be quickly settled. For the moment she has accepted that."

"Then what *is* to be done?" she repeated, walking agitatedly about the room, trying to think clearly and constructively. At last she faced him.

"You said you would be going to Princetown today? I will come with you."

"Miss Conway." His tone was shocked. "You cannot suggest . . . ?"

"I do more than suggest, Dr. Leland, I insist. Armand is in this predicament solely on my sister's account. It is intolerable that I should remain passively here and let him be kept in that dreadful prison awaiting a trial which should never take place. There is a carriage available for hire in the town. I travelled in it yesterday to the concert. Was it only yesterday? It seems ten years ago."

"Miss Conway . . ."

She tilted up her chin. "Are you refusing to take me?"

He drew in his breath slowly. "If I consent to this plan, it will be one of the most indiscreet actions I have ever undertaken."

"Is discretion so very important compared with the wrong done to an innocent man? I had thought better of you than to be concerned for your reputation."

"Do you suppose I am concerned with *that?*" he retorted angrily. "It is you I am thinking of, naturally. You are, after all, a young woman of good family and careful upbringing. If I were to take you with me, unchaperoned . . ."

"Oh, how tiresome you are being!" she exclaimed impatiently. "I declare you sound quite as prim as Aunt Clara." She thought for a moment, then declared with relief, "I have a solution. Mrs. Barlow will come with me, I have no doubt."

The anxious look left his face. "That would certainly meet the difficulty. For indifferent as you may be to convention when Armand's welfare is at stake, someone should have a care for *you* as well."

She gave an exaggerated sigh. "I suppose I should thank you for such concern on my behalf. But, to be sure, I do not take kindly to having my affairs arranged by other people."

He spoke gravely but she saw amusement in his eyes. "I assure you, Miss Conway, I had realised that very early in our acquaintance." He picked up hat and whip. "I will arrange for a carriage to be here at two o'clock this afternoon and for Mrs. Barlow to be collected on the way."

"I will send Phoebe with a note. Dr. Leland, my aunt must know nothing of this plan. She would instantly disapprove and find some way to prevent it."

"And you are determined that nothing shall?" His smile was twisted. "Armand is a fortunate fellow."

"*Fortunate?* How can you say that?"

He turned at the door. "I meant," he said lightly, "in having so charming and resolute a chamion."

She was far too disturbed over what had happened to Armand to realise, until much later, that Paul Leland had actually paid her a compliment.

6

"You should wear something warmer," Mrs. Barlow advised. "There is a mist on the moor which will make it very cold."

Standing in the bright sunshine at the door of Grimstone House, Crissa found this hard to believe, but she went dutifully upstairs and changed the silk pelisse for a green travelling cloak.

"I expected Dr. Leland to be with you," she remarked, joining the older woman in the carriage.

"He is riding to Princetown, visiting a patient on the way. He will join us at Merrivale."

"His practice must cover many miles."

"Indeed it does. He should engage an apprentice to assist him now that he is taking over old Dr. Sawyer's work. But he is an obstinate man and drives himself to the limit of physical endurance. Though what happened three years ago may well explain that."

"Three years ago?" Crissa prompted when her companion lapsed into silence.

"You would not know about that, of course. It was an unfortunate affair. Few people would hold against him that he once failed a patient, but he seems to think he must spend the rest of his life atoning. *And* avoiding any entanglement with a woman. Though, to be sure, if ever a man needed a wife . . ." She glanced out of the window. "You can see now how right I was. You will soon need that rug over your knees. There are few things as penetratingly cold as a Dartmoor mist. And the Transport Board were foolish enough to choose what is known to be the wettest, most wind-swept and mist-shrouded part of the moor on which to build a depot for prisoners of war. Though 'tis said the reason was that Sir Thomas Tyrwhitt wished it to be near his granite quarries so that he might recoup, out of supplying the building materials, the losses he suffered in trying to found an agricultural community in such an unlikely place."

Crissa was disappointed that her companion had not pursued the topic of Paul's past. She did not, however, think it would be seemly to question Mrs. Barlow.

"Phoebe tells me the place was built to house five thousand prisoners. It must be enormous."

"They are crammed in as little space as possible," Mrs. Barlow said with distaste. "They sleep in tiers of hammocks and have no privacy whatsoever. Their every movement in the exercise yard is watched by sentries on the walls, and their only contact with the outside world is the daily market. But unless they augment their allowance by their own ingenuity they have little enough to spend on extra food, or any replacement of clothing. It is quite wonderful what they *do* make. This brooch, for instance, was shaped from a beef bone."

Crissa examined with amazement the ornament fastening her friend's cloak. "It is charming, and so delicately carved. One would not suppose it possible to create such a beautiful article in such sordid surroundings." She shivered. "You were indeed right about the mist. It is like entering another world now we are on the moor."

The carriage was lumbering slowly uphill, lurching sideways as the wheels went in and out of a succession of deep ruts. Beyond the windows drifted streams of grey vapour, obscuring the sun. In a short while they were completely enveloped in mist. All that Crissa could see was a strip of turf at the side of the track and a few clumps of rough heather and gorse.

"Will the coachman find his way?" she asked a little apprehensively.

"It is to be hoped so," Mrs. Barlow answered cheerfully. "When you live on Dartmoor you become used to all kinds of weather—strangers would say, mostly bad. But I would not reside anywhere else, even though it is sometimes a little lonely."

"Do your family not visit you, ma'am?"

"They are too far away, in India, Scotland, New Zealand. Sometimes I wonder whether I shall see any of them ever again." She withdrew a hand from her muff and laid it on Crissa's knee. "That is why, my dear, I am grateful for the company of these young Frenchmen, and yourself. I hope that when your sister is well enough, both you and she will come often to my house."

Crissa turned away. "I think we shall not be here much longer."

"I understood that you were staying some months."

"That was before . . . I mean, it depended on Hetty. It—it is difficult to explain.

Mrs. Barlow's fingers closed over hers. "My dear Clarissa, you do not need to tell me if you do not wish to do so. I can see that you are very troubled, and not only on account of what has happened to Lieutenant de Beauvoir. You are by nature, I am sure, a lively, gay young woman. But more than once during our short meetings I have caught a look of great anxiety in your eyes."

Crissa turned to her companion. The widow's face showed such kindness and concern that her resolution to keep silent was swept aside.

"I would so like to tell you, ma'am, if you will promise to keep the matter to yourself. It is my sister's story, you see, not mine."

When Crissa finished her explanation, Mrs. Barlow's brown eyes were full of sympathy.

"Poor child! As if she had not enough to suffer by losing her husband. How cruel some fathers can be."

"I do not think Papa would consider himself cruel. Hetty has greatly injured his pride, you see, and that she dared to defy him shocked him dreadfully. If it had been myself he would have borne it much more easily. For I was always the one expected to cause trouble."

"I find that so difficult to believe, as I did Miss Conway's assertion that you defied her at every turn."

"I am afraid it is true."

"You do not defy me, child. You went most dutifully to change your cloak."

Crissa's eyes widened. "But *your* thought was en-

133

tirely for my comfort. Why should I resent that?"

Mrs. Barlow laughed. "And your aunt's commands are not for your comfort?"

"Indeed they are not," Crissa answered feelingly. "Oh dear, I suppose it is wrong of me to say that. I should not criticise her."

Mrs. Barlow squeezed her hand. "Miss Conway is a most worthy lady and endowed with great courage. But she has, I think, little understanding of young people, and it sounds to me as though her brother is cast in the same mould. Clarissa, it is not for me to interfere in this family affair. But if you need help at any time and you think I may be of the slightest assistance or comfort to you, promise that you will come to me."

"I will indeed, ma'am," Crissa promised warmly. "And I thank you with all my heart. For although I am quite determined that Hetty shall not be parted from her baby, yet I do not know how it may be accomplished."

The carriage, which had been slowly descending a very steep hill, came to a halt. Through the mist Crissa saw a horseman approaching. Mrs. Barlow let down her window to greet Paul. His hair, beneath the curved brim of his hat, was curling in the damp, and his eyelashes were beaded with moisture.

"We could scarce have a worse day for such a journey," he said. "Would it not be better for you ladies to turn back and try again tomorrow?"

"I am not so easily put off," Mrs. Barlow asserted stoutly. "Provided the coachman can find his way, we are snug enough in here. Clarissa, are you of the same mind?"

"Indeed, yes. After your description of the prison I cannot bear to think of Armand shut up there a moment longer than necessary. Will he be allowed to return with us, do you suppose?"

"I doubt it," Paul replied. "However much the Governor may sympathise when he hears the true story, I think he may have to apply to the Transport Office for Armand's release. The regulations . . ."

"Oh, rules and regulations!" Crissa exclaimed in disgust. "He is innocent. He should therefore be set free immediately."

Paul exchanged an amused look with Mrs. Barlow. "I have a suspicion the Emperor Napoleon would have been vanquished long ago if Miss Conway had the ordering of the war. 'Tis not to be wondered at that Miss Clara has had to take to her bed." He hunched his shoulders. "Shall we move on? It's deuced cold astride a horse today."

Crissa thrust her hands beneath the rug and gripped her fingers tightly together. Her cheeks were burning. Mrs. Barlow chuckled.

"You must not mind Dr. Leland's tongue, my dear. It is not his way to flatter women. You might even regard what he said as complimentary. But naturally you prefer Armand's pleasantries. Are you in love with him, Clarissa?"

Taken aback by the directness of the question, Crissa hesitated. "I—I do not rightly know. A little, perhaps. But then, I fall in love so easily. When we left Dartmouth I thought I should be quite lost without a young man called Harry. But in truth I have scarce thought of him these last few days. Does that sound very dreadful to you, ma'am?"

"Not in the least. Only it is to be hoped that

one day you will cease flirting and settle down with a man to whom you have truly given your heart."

"Oh, I hope so, too," Crissa said fervently. "Sometimes it worries me a little that I have not yet done so. For I am already twenty-one."

Her companion laughed. "You must not mind my being amused, my dear. You remind me of my daughter Sarah."

"Then I shall not mind in the least. For that would suggest you bear me some affection."

"You may be sure of that."

They toiled up a long, steep hill, the straps of the carriage creaking under the strain, stopping at intervals to rest the horses. At the top they turned right-handed and Mrs. Barlow leaned forward.

"We are almost there. And, strangely enough, it is a little clearer here."

Crissa peered out of the window. Through a break in the mist she could see the high encircling walls of the prison, and tall, rectangular buildings, stark as the moorland waste all about them. They passed a house, then drew up before the main gate. Its archway was formed of huge granite blocks. On the centre one, two Latin words were inscribed, and below, on either side, oil lamps hung above noticeboards. Through the arch she could see yet another massive gate and before each of them sentries were patrolling. Involuntarily she shuddered.

"You may well look dismayed," remarked Mrs. Barlow. "When those iron gates clang to behind a man, he must assuredly feel that all hope is shut out. Yet it is said that many of the prisoners achieve a passable life for themselves, especially the ones they call 'Les Lords.' Armand will be amongst them,

I imagine, having been apprehended as a broke parole and lodged in the Petty Officers' block. If they have money they even engage servants from amongst the less fortunate prisoners."

"Then it is not so bad as I had supposed," Crissa said in relief.

"Things never are so bad for the privileged, my dear. But for the others, there is much hardship. In the winter of 1809 there was an outbreak of measles which, added to the dreadful weather, accounted for many deaths. Yet, strangely enough, the ones who are most healthy are those who gamble away everything so that they exist half-starved and half-naked, sleeping in packed rows on the bare stone floors. Even if they are given clothes and bedding and money, they persist in gambling it all away and continuing to live in squalor beyond our comprehension."

"How do you know so much about the conditions?" Crissa enquired.

"Some of our townsfolk come with their produce to the daily market and naturally they see and learn of these things, and gossip about them. And Dr. Leland, of course, is much concerned with the plight of the prisoners and does what he can unofficially to help them. Ah, here he comes."

He was frowning as he reined in beside the carriage window. "It seems everything is against us. Both the Governor, and the doctor whom I know, are away for the day. I have spoken to one of the officers in charge of the guard and he has gone to enquire if there is anybody in authority whom we may see."

After what seemed to Crissa an interminable wait,

the outer gate was opened and they drove through, halting again in the military road which ran between high walls encircling the prisoners' quarters. Beyond the iron railings Crissa could discern shadowy figures moving about in a yard, some in the regulation yellow jackets showing up more clearly. Glancing up, she saw two of the sentries on the inner wall, the colours of their uniforms dulled by the mist.

Paul came again to the carriage, this time on foot. His face was as gloomy as the weather.

"What is it?" Mrs. Barlow asked. "Has this tedious journey been in vain?"

"I have been talking to the clerk."

"Well?" Crissa prompted impatiently, but her heart sank at his expression.

"I wish I could give you better news," he answered reluctantly.

"Then they will not release Armand at once?"

"They *cannot* release him—yet."

"Why not? Because of this ridiculous ruling about consulting the Transport Office? Really, I declare . . ."

"It is more than that, Miss Conway. Armand himself has caused his stay to be prolonged."

Crissa and her companion stared at him in dismay.

"You had best explain," Mrs. Barlow said.

Paul sighed heavily. "One cannot blame him, I suppose. In the same situation I should myself have been equally resentful towards Captain d'Aubois. But *we* are not so much given to duelling as the French."

*"Duelling!"* The word was uttered by both women at once.

"It is quite common in the prisons."

"How can that be?" Mrs. Barlow demanded. "We are not to suppose, surely, that they are allowed to retain their swords or pistols?"

Paul shook his head. "The French are notoriously clever at improvisation. Even makeshift foils are not beyond them."

Crissa leaned forward. "So Armand fought a duel."

"And severely wounded his opponent. If the Captain recovers, Armand may be given some minor punishment, but it will most likely be regarded as an affair of honour between gentlemen—once his innocence last night is proved, that is."

"And if this Captain does not recover?"

Paul's frown deepened. "Then it is a matter for the civil court. Armand would be tried for manslaughter before the Assizes at Exeter."

"Oh, why was he so foolish?" Crissa exclaimed. "He must have been certain of quick release. Why throw away the chance like that?"

"You should know by now that to Armand his honour is everything. For the wrong done to him last night by his fellow officer, there would be only one redress in his opinion."

"So now he will be kept here?" She shivered again as she glanced up at the high wall, at the iron railings shutting out hope.

"For the time, yes."

"We can do nothing?"

Again he shook his head regretfully. "Except to pray for Captain d'Aubois' recovery."

For a few minutes she sat with tightly clasped

hands, staring hopelessly at the sentry on his high platform. Then she straightened her shoulders. "No, I will not be put off. It is entirely on my sister's account that poor Armand is here at all. It would be the greatest weakness not to attempt some action, however small, on his behalf."

Paul glanced enquiringly at Mrs. Barlow.

She said, "I think Clarissa is right. Certainly no harm can be done by an interview with whoever is in authority in the Governor's absence."

Paul shrugged. "I will see what can be arranged."

Ten minutes later they were received by the prison clerk in the Governor's office.

"My father is a lawyer and a gentleman of some standing in Dartmouth and Totnes," Crissa said firmly. "Therefore I think you may accept what I shall tell you regarding Lieutenant de Beauvoir without questioning its veracity."

The clerk, his face impassive, motioned her to a chair and set another for Mrs. Barlow. Paul stood to one side. When he had finished writing down Crissa's statement the clerk looked up.

"This is exactly the explanation Lieutenant de Beauvoir gave us, Miss Conway. But naturally the agent at Tavistock had to take precautions in the circumstances."

"The circumstances being that a fellow officer lied and that he was believed, presumably since he is of higher rank," she said angrily.

"That is scarcely for me to comment on."

"I never heard of such an outrageous miscarriage of justice," she went on, unconsciously using words her father might have chosen. "To arrest a man, in uniform, outside a doctor's house, and pretend to believe that he is making an attempt to escape. Why, I can scarcely credit anyone being so stupid."

The clerk said hesitantly, "With due respect to your reasoning, ma'am, I think your father would have taken the view that information had been lodged which had to be proved or disproved."

"And now it has been disproved," she said airily, "there is no sensible reason why Arm—why Monsieur de Beauvoir should not be released."

"I am afraid there is," the man argued patiently. "Did not Dr. Leland explain the matter to you?"

"He mentioned some nonsense about a duel. As if two French officers fighting each other can be of the slightest significance to anyone but themselves."

"If Lieutenant de Beauvoir's opponent should die, it becomes a capital offence."

She lifted her hands, then let them drop on her lap. Exasperatedly she exclaimed, "Such a ridiculous attitude is no more than one would expect, I suppose. Men are judged the masters of logic. To my mind they waste a considerable amount of time over matters of no importance whatsoever!"

The clerk caught Paul's eye, then bent his head to hide a smile. "May I ask, Miss Conway, what you consider the most important matter at this moment?"

"You may, and I will tell you," she answered with asperity. "That this officer, whose honour has never for a moment been in question, should be freed as soon as possible. And," she added, tilting her chin, "that we should be allowed to see him, to assure him that he has not been forgotten by his friends whilst he is in this dreadful place."

Mrs. Barlow put a hand on her arm. "My dear, I think you should not . . ."

"Forgive me, madam," the clerk interrupted. "But if Miss Conway makes such a request I must deal with it." He looked speculatively at Crissa. "May I ask if you are related to this officer?"

"No. Certainly I am not. But he is the grandson of an English friend of my aunt in whose house he is lodged. That is where I met him, only a few weeks ago. This I have already explained to you. Any other construction you may put upon our acquaintance is unfounded and, I may say, impertinent."

A sudden movement made her glance towards Pal. For a moment the expression of admiration on his face disconcerted her. Then she turned back to the clerk.

"Your answer, sir," she demanded.

He shuffled his papers together and stood up. "The matter does not rest with me. I shall have to confer with the officer in charge of the guard."

"Then pray do so, at once." Suddenly she realised that her tactics might have been wrong. Smiling at the clerk, she said in a voice to match, "If you would be so kind, that is, sir. I—we are naturally most anxious about the fate of a gentleman who has behaved, in difficult circumstances, with the utmost rectitude. I thought that if we might see him, if only for a few minutes, to reassure him . . ." Deliberately she allowed her eyes to complete the request.

The clerk cleared his throat, made her a little bow. "I will do my best, Miss Conway, to procure you an interview with Lieutenant de Beauvoir."

Crissa rose to her feet as the young Frenchman entered the office. "Armand, why is your arm in a sling?" she asked at once. "Were you also injured in this duel? Oh, I remember. Your shoulder was hurt last night. How then could you handle a foil?"

He bowed formally to both ladies and greeted Paul warmly before replying. His voice had a bitter note.

"When I was wounded aboard my ship, I forgot that I had a left arm. The fact did not escape my memory today."

"You fought left-handed?" Paul asked in astonishment.

"I did, and won." Despite his immaculate uniform, the fair hair so carefully brushed, Crissa saw a change in him. His mouth and eyes looked more like Paul's than those of the debonair young officer who had kissed her under the moonlit trees the previous evening.

He said stiffly, "It was good of you to come, Mrs. Barlow, Miss Conway."

"What else would you expect?" Crissa asked. "I cannot express how angry I was when I heard what had happened. That you should have been subjected to—to this"—she gestured towards the sentry-guarded walls beyond the window—"in return for the kindness you did last night."

His face softened as he asked, "How is *la petite* Hetty?"

"She is well, but rather weak."

"And the baby? It is born?"

"Yes, and safely, thanks to Dr. Leland."

He made an expressive gesture with his hands and his eyes lit up. He was again the Armand she knew. "You see? I told you, you could have no better physician. You will give your sister my congratulations and good wishes?"

She said gently, "When you return, Armand, I am sure Hetty will be glad to receive them personally."

His blue eyes widened. "You mean she will no longer avoid me?"

"I think not, after what you did for her last night."

Mrs. Barlow rose and glanced at Paul. "Dr. Leland, I think I shall be warmer in the carriage. Would you be so kind as to escort me?"

Crossing the room to her side, Paul laid a hand on Armand's arm. "Rest assured, you will be back amongst us very soon. If Miss Conway had her way, we would bustle you into the carriage and abscond with you at once."

Armand asked, when he and Crissa were alone, "He teases you?"

"Yes, a little."

"You do not mind?"

"I—I am learning not to."

"That is good to hear, Crissa. I do not like my friends to be enemies." He laughed shortly. "Though that is a foolish remark since you two are English and I, in fact, the enemy."

"I can never think of you as such. As for Dr. Leland, he could not have been kinder or more skilful. I am sure that Hetty and her child owe their lives to him. And to you. Oh, Armand . . ." Her voice faltered.

He took hold of her hand. "Do not distress yourself on my account, Crissa. If I had not been so foolish as to move towards your sister so hastily last evening she would not have fallen."

"You cannot be blamed for her fall. Not even she would do that."

"She has really changed? She does not hate me quite so much?"

"Now that her child is born, I believe it will be different. She will forget this bitterness and resentment which is so contrary to her nature. And she will be as sorry as I am that you were foolish enough to fight this duel and so prejudice your chance of immediate release."

The hard look returned to his eyes. He released her hand and turned a little away. "*Pardon, mademoiselle,* but I do not consider it foolish to avenge myself on a fellow officer who has betrayed my honour."

"He will be punished for trying to escape. Was that not enough?"

She was startled by the look he gave her. "He will be punished for breaking his parole, for the stain upon his own honour. That is in no way concerned with the injury he did to mine."

She was confronted by an attitude which was wholly masculine. Yet though she thought it ridiculous, she admired him for it. His attraction for her had been that of a charming, agreeable young man who enjoyed to the full the pleasures life afforded him, and made the best of the misfortunes. She saw now beyond this façade he had adopted to make tolerable the life he was leading. His chosen path had been that of a serving officer, prepared to face the dangers of war and the sea itself. Instead he was being forced to pass his days aimlessly with the circumscribed limits of a mile in each direction of a small country town. She felt a new regard for him. She said gently, "I am sorry if I offended you."

At once he smiled. "It is just that you are a woman and do not understand. To a Frenchman, and especially to an officer, his honour is everything. Though . . ." he broke off, frowning. "Though you would not think so if you entered *le Petit Cautionnement* here. It is full of officers who have broken their parole. Yet most of them seem entirely without shame and amuse themselves gambling or music making or dancing. They dress *à la mode*, even affecting ruffles and frills as if they were at a ball instead of in a prison." He gritted his teeth. "*Ma foi*, I would like to teach some of them a lesson as I taught le Capitaine d'Aubois."

Her anxiety returned. "Armand, if he should die, you will be forced to stand trial. Do you know that?"

"Yes. But I cannot see why. The duel was entirely a matter between ourselves and was fought within the accepted code of rules."

"I do not see why, either," she confessed. "But then, I never have understood legal matters. My father has often lost patience with me, though Hetty seems to grasp his meaning at once."

Armand threw back his head and laughed.

"I cannot conceive why that should amuse you," she said with some asperity.

"Delightful Crissa." He took her hand and held it against his chest. "I can well imagine your poor Papa solemnly describing to you some finer point of law, the while your gaze is straying out of the window in search of any of your admirers who happens to be passing."

For a moment she feigned offence. Then she laughed. "How well you know me! Yet you must not believe I am always concerned with young men—or—or seeking amusement."

His fingers caressed hers. "I do not believe it, *ma chère* Clareesa. Have I not seen your devotion to your sister, your concern on her behalf? And have you not come here today, facing a drive which must have been most unpleasant, entering this place of gloom to plead on my behalf? Yes, I know you, Crissa, perhaps because, as I told you before, we are so alike. To the world we show the gay face, *n'est-ce pas?* But beneath . . ."

He leaned towards her. At that moment there was a knock at the door and the clerk entered to tell her it was time to leave. In another second Armand would undoubtedly have kissed her as he had done beneath the trees last night. Although she would greatly have enjoyed the experience, she was not at all sure that it would have been wise. To fall lightly in love with a handsome French officer was one thing. To allow herself to become more deeply involved with a man who was, after all, an enemy and would return to his own country after the war, was quite another.

"I will write to you, Monsieur de Beauvoir," she promised formally as she went towards the door. "You may believe that everything will be done to procure your speedy release. If there is anything you require . . ."

He answered with equally cool politeness. "I

should be obliged, mademoiselle, if arrangements could be made to send me some money."

Impulsively she opened her reticule. "I could . . ." Then she saw the clerk's eyes upon her. Hastily she drew the strings together. "That is, I will ask Dr. Leland to attend to the matter. *Au revoir, monsieur.*"

## 7

"It is such a warm afternoon I think I shall go for a walk," said Crissa, putting the baby, which she had been nursing, in the carved cradle in which his grandfather had been rocked to sleep. "Phoebe will stay with you, dear."

"There is not the slightest need," Hetty assured her. "I am much stronger now and am so enjoying sitting out a little. I am not happy when you walk alone. Why not take Phoebe with you?"

"Phoebe will stay with you," Crissa said decisively.

"How you cosset me, you and Dr. Leland. I have completely changed my opinion of him. He is so gentle and kind, you would not suppose him to be the fierce man we encountered on the Plymouth road. He was here quite twenty minutes this morning just talking to me."

"Then you were favoured," Crissa remarked with asperity. "Since the day we visited Armand in prison he has scarce addressed more than a dozen words to me."

Hetty looked up in surprise. "How strange! For

I think he has grown to like you quite well. Is there no further news of Armand?"

Crissa shook her head regretfully. "None, since his letter of two days ago in which he said Captain d'Aubois' condition appears unchanged. It is ten days now," she added impatiently. "Surely they must know whether he will live or die. The suspense for us is bad enough. It must be nigh unbearable for Armand."

Hetty rocked the cradle with her foot. "Do you think he will ever forgive me for the way I treated him?"

"Of course he will. He understood perfectly. And he so much appreciated your writing to the Governor on his behalf."

"It was the least I could do, since he is in the prison entirely on my account. When he does return —as I am sure he must before long—I shall feel very shy at meeting him."

"Armand will soon put you at your ease. These Frenchmen certainly have the most charming manners."

"And one of them more than the rest? Crissa, would you ever think of marrying Armand should he ask you?"

Crissa paused as she reached for her cloak hanging in the wardrobe. "I do not know, Hetty. It is not a decision that could be made in a hurry. For one thing, Mrs. Barlow has mentioned that such marriages are considered invalid in France at present. And then, of course, Papa would be sure to raise objections."

"But you are very fond of him?"

"Yes. He is charming and agreeable and courageous. But . . ." She frowned as she fastened her cloak. "I think perhaps we are too alike in many ways. And—strange as this may sound," she went on, turning to face her sister, "although I dearly love my own way, I do not always wish to have it."

Hetty laughed. "That sounds like a conundrum. What *can* you mean?"

Crissa's frown deepened. "I find it difficult to explain. But I believe that Armand, like Harry, would oblige me in everything. And I do not think that would be very good for me," she ended in a flash of self-revelation.

"Well, I am sure I cannot understand you," Hetty said, gazing fondly down at her son. "For I declare I would be only too happy for my husband to oblige me all the time. Oh, Crissa . . ."

"What is it?" her sister asked in alarm at her tone.

"If only I *had* a husband." Hetty pressed her hands to her cheeks. But as Crissa put an arm around her shoulders, she sat up straight and said in a firmer voice, "No, I must not be so weak. Doctor Leland said it is bad for me and the baby, for I shall not be able to feed him well enough if I am upset. And I am thankful to be doing so instead of handing him over to that farm girl, well as she performed her duties. Go for your walk, dearest. You spend far too much time dancing attendance upon me and Aunt Clara. And I do not need Phoebe to sit here if she has tasks to do."

It was not, however, merely that she should sit with Hetty that Crissa insisted on Phoebe going immediately to the bedroom. She and the maid had a tacit undersanding that Hetty's baby should never be left alone. For Crissa had the constant fear that the child would be snatched away. Phoebe's notion was that Martha would admit the "witch" to the house to put the evil eye on the baby. Ridiculous as both fancies might be, neither Crissa nor the maid proposed to take any chances. So night and day they constituted themselves as bodyguards.

As she started down the stairs Crissa heard Aunt Clara calling her from along the passage. Impatiently she went to answer the summons. The old lady also was sitting out for a little while each day, in a rocking chair in the window embrasure, a rug over her knees, her spectacles clamped firmly to her nose.

"Did you write to your father?" she demanded as Crissa entered.

"Yes, ma'am, nine days ago. Perhaps he is from home. He often is."

"What did you say to him? Really, I think I should have insisted on seeing your letter."

Crissa sighed audibly. "I informed him that Hetty's child had been born prematurely; that she was rather weak and the baby naturally very small, but that the physician saw no reason for anxiety."

"Is that all you wrote?" Aunt Clara's eyes, demanding the truth, were watching her relentlessly.

Crissa hesitated, but there was no escaping that look. "I added that it was wonderful to see the joy with which Hetty regarded her child. I told him that her baby was her only consolation for losing the husband she loved."

"Did you suppose that would carry any weight with your father?"

Crissa bent her head. "No. But I felt it had to be written. I thought . . ." She lifted her head and looked defiantly at her aunt. "I hoped against all reason that now Papa knew he had a grandson he might conceivably relent."

"So you are aware of what he proposed?"

"Of course. He made it perfectly plain to me before we left Dartmouth that Hetty would not be allowed to keep her child. I did not know he could be so monstrously cruel."

"*Clarissa!*"

Crissa did not heed the warning. "In your heart, Aunt Clara, do *you* not think it cruel?"

The old lady drew in a sharp breath and twitched fiercely at her grey skirt. "I am not to be catechised by you, miss. In any case, neither your opinion nor mine will make the slighest difference. Your father must be obeyed."

"By Hetty, yes. But not by me. I am of age, which both you and he seem to forget."

"So you intend to defy him?"

"If he cannot be moved by pity or by the warm regard he has always had for Hetty, yes, I do."

"And how will your defiance benefit your sister, may I ask?"

Crissa moved restlessly about the room. "In truth, I do not know. But I will tell you this." She swung round and faced the old woman. "If that baby is taken, he will have to be snatched forcibly from my arms or Phoebe's. For neither of us leaves him untended day or night."

Her aunt's eyes narrowed and she regarded her niece over her spectacles for a few moments. Then she said tartly, "I cannot think why it had to be Henrietta who was so indiscreet. Had it been you, which seems a deal more likely, I assume you would have found a way out of such a predicament?"

Crissa ignored the jibe. "There is no predicament except what Papa has made of it," she said coldly. "And as you say, I would have found a way. Even now, had I the means, I would take Hetty with me and ..."

"Take care what you are saying! You know well enough that my first loyalty is to my brother."

"And you will repeat to him everything I have said? Oh, you have no need to warn me." Suddenly her defiance slipped from her like a cloak. She said hopelessly, "In my heart I am aware that however fiercely I may protest and utter rebellious words, there is in the end no way in which I may save Hetty from this further heartbreak if Papa is set on it."

Although the October afternoon held a rare warmth, and the sunlight sparkled on the river and intensified the colours of each late blossom of heather and scabious and harebell, there was no lightness in Crissa's step as she emerged from the lane on the turnpike road. She hesitated, then turned left, away from the town, and, after a short while, branched off to the right along a track leading to the packhorse bridge and up on to the moor.

She felt weighed down with anxieties. She could not get out of her mind the picture she had formed of the grim grey prison where Armand was still held. Surely fate would not be so cruel as to let Captain d'Aubois die and Armand be committed for trial at Exeter Assizes? It would be so grossly unfair. But was not Papa's treatment of Hetty grossly unfair? And no kind fate had stepped in to prevent that.

She longed for Armand's gay company. Yet she could not help feeling that her behaviour may have been a little indiscreet. After all, he was French, and Frenchmen were notoriously gallant and amorous without any serious intentions.

Away to her right there was a glitter as sunlight fell upon metal of some kind. Three men were standing before the gate of Mrs. Barlow's house. Even at this distance she recognised the red and white uniform of militiamen and hoped that the two young officers whom Mrs. Barlow entertained so often had not been involved in any trouble.

She continued up the track, stepping carefully although she had put on her kid boots, for the surface was muddy and uneven. The murmur of the river sounded from the valley. A few late bees sought the gorse blossoms. Browsing sheep raised their heads to watch her nervously as she passed, their jaws working methodically the while.

She glanced back. The road was hidden, and the town itself, and any sign of a house. She had never before come so far on to the open moor as this. But in daylight, with the sun shining and only the tiniest of clouds away to the west, it was not the least frightening. In fact, it seemed to Crissa a place of the utmost peace, and soon her spirits lifted and she looked around her with delight at the beauty of her surroundings. She even smiled to herself as she remembered how on the second night at Grimstone she had heard a dog howling across the moor and half believed Phoebe's tales of wish hounds and a coach of bones with a headless driver. Why, only this morning Phoebe had spun another of her fantastic tales, some story of a farmer wounding a hare in a hind leg with his gun, and the very next day the old crone whom Phoebe had confronted with the sign of the cross had been seen to have a pronounced limp.

"And 'tis well known that witches can take on the forms of hares when they've a mind to," the superstitious maid had declared.

Lost in her musings, Crissa was startled by the sound of hooves behind her. Thinking it might be a wild pony, she scrambled hastily off the track into the rough heather. But it was Paul who appeared over the ridge.

He reined in at sight of her. "Why, Miss Conway, I did not expect to see *you* walking alone on the moor. It is not often strangers to the district venture so far from the turnpike road." He glanced over his shoulder, frowning. "I should not go much further, though. There will be rain before long."

"Oh, surely not? The sky is almost cloudless."

"You must allow me to know the weather signs better than you. I assure you that by evening you will be glad to be indoors. As you may be aware by now, a Dartmoor storm is both fierce and sudden. And there is no shelter here save for the tinners' old buildings down by the river, as I know from bitter experience."

"Are you visiting a patient?" she asked. "There would not seem to be a habitation for miles around."

He pointed with his whip. "There is a smallholding beyond that outcrop of rock. Though how they make a living I find hard to understand. The eldest boy, who should have known better, pulled the pony's tail and got kicked in the chest and two broken ribs for his trouble."

"What a lonely place to live."

"It is indeed. Not a sight of a neighbour, and cut off completely when the snow comes. But there are many farms on the moor more isolated than that one. Magpie Farm, for instance, two miles off the Okehampton road. When the Silver Dagger mines were working, they had some sight of other human beings. Nowadays, they don't see a stranger for weeks. It's no wonder they invited me to dinner for the sake of a talk. Though, to be sure, 'tis often how I get paid for my services."

"And you have to visit these lonely places, in all weathers, if they send for you," she reflected with a new appreciation of his work.

He smiled ruefully. "There are times when I expect to end as a patient myself. If it were not for this sure-footed creature"—he patted his mount's neck —"I doubt if I'd find my way home on some nights."

With startling clarity she pictured him plodding back, late at night, to his house in Tavistock, cold, wet, dead tired. Who would welcome him and give him comfort? Did his housekeeper wait up, whatever the hour? Was there a manservant to care for his horse? Or did he have that task to perform also before he could seek warmth and food and his bed?

He said, "You are looking pensive, Miss Conway. Have I said something to disturb you?"

Her answer was spoken impulsively. "I was thinking that a doctor, more than most men, needs a wife."

The words were scarcely spoken before she regretted them. His mouth and eyes took on a hard look; his hands tightened on the reins.

"I had that thought once, Miss Conway. And it all but ruined my career. I do not propose to repeat such folly. Even to speak of it should remind me that I must be on my way. I bid you good-day, and I pray you to heed my warning about the weather."

She stared after him as he set off along the track. She felt anger at being snubbed but, at the same time, blamed herself for broaching a subject which she had been warned more than once he wished to avoid. What had happened to make him feel this antagonism towards women? If only Mrs. Barlow had revealed more in the carriage on the way to Princetown. He could be so kind, so sympathetic. But as a doctor only? "As a man I am not so understanding," he had told her. Yet he was both the doctor and the man. How could he separate the one from the other, and why did he want to?

Crissa glanced at the sky. She did not believe that it would rain, at least not for hours yet. Paul probably did not approve of her walking alone on the moor and that was his way of persuading her to return. In another ten minutes, she resolved, she would turn back, but not before. She would just go to the top of the next rise, from where she might catch a glimpse of the smallholding to which Paul had ridden. And if he should come upon her as he returned, he should see that she was not to be given orders by him. Except, of course, when he was the doctor.

Her thoughts seemed as jumbled as the rocks on the skyline. She had sufficient problems, with Armand and Hetty and her father's reaction to the birth of his grandson, without giving any time to the enigma of Paul Leland. But it was he who occupied her mind as she went on up the hill.

There was a clatter of stones behind. She turned to see what had caused it. Climbing up the slope from the river was a bent figure in a tattered black cloak, a shawl concealing hair and face. Crissa gasped as she recognised Phoebe's black witch. The old woman lifted her head, listening, then turned towards Crissa. For a long moment the startling black eyes held her gaze. There was a strange prickly feeling along her spine, and she shivered. She wanted to turn away, but could not. It was the crone who moved first. Uttering a thin, nasal sound which might have been laughter, she scrambled on to the track and made off in the direction from which Crissa had come. And she was limping. Crissa tried to tell herself that her reaction had been understandable. This was a lonely part, after all, and so quiet that sounds as ordinary as the rattle of a stone, the clop of hooves or the shrill whinny of a pony were magnified to such an extent that they became startling in their sharpness.

But she had been startled many times in her life and never felt as she had done a few minutes since. Never before had she been afraid of an old woman, old and lame and probably quite harmless. Why, the old creature had not even come towards her. She made off in as great a hurry as her limp allowed. All the same . . .

Crissa stared along the track which was the route she must take, and saw with dismay that Paul had been right. Clouds were gathering in the west, high, bulging and ominous. A breeze stirred the dry stalks of heather and whipped at the hem of her thin cloak. She walked a few paces, then stopped. Suppose she should wait for Paul to escort her back? But he would not welcome her company, for he was mounted and she on foot, and she could scarcely see him lifting her to his saddle like a knight rescuing some damsel in distress. She laughed at the thought, but her laughter did not sound quite natural. She walked on again. The thought of following the same path as that old crone, of perhaps being confronted with her round the next bend, did not appeal to Crissa in the least. She chided herself for being so weak. After all, even if she were foolish enough to believe there was something sinister about the old woman, she had but to follow Phoebe's example and make the sign of the cross. It could be done quite easily under cover of her cloak so that such weakness need not be witnessed. But, in that case, would it work?

She thrust up her chin and walked resolutely forward. It was ridiculous to pay the least attention to the superstitions of a maidservant and simple country folk. As if an old woman should limp because a farmer had wounded a hare in its leg. It was utterly . . .

The sudden bleat of a sheep came from the path just ahead. And from the west, a low rumbling. Both sounds stopped Crissa in her tracks, heart thudding painfully. She glanced behind her, then stared unblinking at the path ahead. Nothing moved, save the bracken stirring in the freshening breeze. There was no sound now except the rustle of dry heather stalks and the tinkle of a moorland stream, and the faint murmur of the river amongst the trees. The river. If she were to make her way down to it, she must surely find a path which would lead her to the packhorse bridge.

Without pausing to reason further—and indeed her powers of reasoning seemed to have deserted her—she started down the steep hillside, slipping and stumbling. Her legs were scratched by gorse and the sharp stalks of heather. Small stones rattled from beneath her feet. A few scattered sheep bounded away in fright, bleating loudly. As she reached the bottom of the slope, there came a roll of thunder. She found a path, trodden hard but made difficult by tree roots and moss-covered stones. It was darker down here, but the trees gave her a sense of protection. The river, bubbling and frothing amongst the debris of previous storms, had a companionable sound. Deliberately she forced herself to stand still and look about her, ashamed of the panic which had sent her headlong down the hill.

Set back from the river was a tumbledown building which had been made of granite boulders, and roughly thatched. It was, she supposed, the shelter formerly used by the tinners which Paul had mentioned. She walked towards it, wondering how long since it had been used. Then, above the noise of the river, she heard another sound. Fearfully she glanced around her. Where had that cry come from? An animal, perhaps, hidden in the undergrowth? It came again, and this time she knew from where. The wail, as of a departing spirit, came from the ruin of the tinners' shelter.

As if all the hobgoblins of the moor were after her, Crissa picked up her skirts and ran along the path. In her haste she tripped over a tree root and fell, hitting her elbow against a boulder. She crouched, cradling her arm, rocking backwards and forwards, unable to stop herself crying out.

Then, quite clearly, she heard a human voice.

"*Au secours! Aidez-moi. Pour l'amour de Dieu, aidez-moi.*"

Crissa bit her lip hard. Again she heard the words, more loudly this time. Still nursing her elbow, she rose to her feet. Cautiously she retraced her steps to within a few yards of the ruined building.

"Is someone there?" she called nervously.

"*Si. Si. Ici!*"

She stood hesitant, every instinct urging her to run as fast as she could, away from this eerie place. Yet the voice was unmistakeably human. Suddenly the fact that the call had been in French penetrated her numbed brain. She was so used by now to hearing that language spoken that she had not at once realised the implication of its use in this place, far beyond the mile limit prescribed for parole prisoners. What was a Frenchman doing here?

The cries were repeated, sounding desperate now, and interspersed with a sound like sobbing.

Crissa glanced around her and picked up a fallen branch which looked strong yet light enough for her to use should the necessity arise. Carefully she stepped over the fallen stones at the entrance to the hut.

"Who is there? Where are you?" she called, peering into the dark interior.

"*Ici, madame.*"

"I cannot see you." She tried to make her voice sound deeper and sterner. "And pray speak English. I do not understand French very well."

The answer came with obvious difficulty. "I have —little English. Do not have fear, I am—*blessé. Comprenez—vous?* My leg, it is no good."

Her eyes were becoming accustomed to the darkness. Faintly, a few feet away, she could distinguish a figure. She pulled aside a trailing canopy of ivy and light fell on the crumpled form of a man lying on the littered floor. Gripping her stick firmly, she moved forward.

She saw then that she had indeed nothing to fear. The Frenchman was younger than any she had seen, a mere boy, in fact. His black hair was tousled, his face white and drawn. He wore rough country clothes. But what she noticed above all else was the unnatural angle of his left leg, and his hands were clenched so hard that it seemed the knuckles would burst through the skin.

She put down her stick and knelt beside him. "Who are you? And what has happened?"

"I . . ." He shook his head helplessly.

She tried again. "You are—*vous êtes un prisonnier de guerre?*"

"*Oui.*"

"You have . . . ?" She did not know the word for escape. "*Vous êtes fugitif?*" she asked instead.

"*Oui.*" He went into a long explanation, in which the words "depot" and "Princetown" were all she understood.

"Princetown?" she repeated in astonishment. "You have escaped from the prison there?"

He nodded, then cried out in pain as he made an incautious movement.

Crissa looked more closely at his leg. Her first fear was confirmed. It was certainly broken. There was nothing she could do to aid him, then, save go for assistance. But to do that would mean . . .

In the light let in between the ivy she saw an old tin mug standing amongst the stones. She rose and picked it up.

"I will get you some water to drink and think how I may best help you. *Vous comprenez?*"

"*Oui, mademoiselle. Merci.*"

But as she picked her way out of the ruined building, she heard his voice, like a frightened child's. "You will—come back?"

"Of course. *Certainement.*"

She went swiftly to the river and rinsed the mug, then filled it with the cold clear water. When she returned the boy was moaning, but he stopped as she entered. Kneeling beside him on the rough ground, she held the mug while he drank thirstily.

When he had done she said slowly, "Try to understand. I must go for help. You need a doctor."

He nodded resignedly. "*Mais maintenant, alors, les soldats—et une rentrée encore à la prison.*"

The hopelessness in his voice struck at Crissa's heart. He was so utterly in her hands. And he was too young to go to war and be made prisoner in a foreign land; too young to spend years in the horrible depot at Princetown. Involuntarily she shuddered as she recalled those high granite walls, the spiked iron railings, and the sentries posted every few yards. This boy, of course, would not be an officer. His place would be in one of the casernes which housed hundreds of men crammed together like animals in the market. Whatever she did for him now would only help to send him back to that living hell. If there were only some other way . . .

Suddenly there did seem to be a way. She must fetch a doctor, and that doctor would be Paul Leland. And Paul was already near at hand, if she were quick enough. And he was the French prisoners' friend. How far did that friendship go? Was there any truth in those rumours of his helping prisoners to escape, despite his denial?

She rose. "I am going to fetch a doctor," she said clearly. "Do not be afraid. I will come back."

He caught her hand and clung to it like a child, then held it against his cheek. "*Merci, mademoiselle. Vouse êtes très gentille.* I am not good at being *fugitif.*"

Breathlessly Crissa scrambled up the hillside, her feet slipping on heather and loose stones. Her cloak caught on a gorse bush. Impatiently she pulled it free, hearing the rasp of torn silk. The thunderstorm seemed to have moved away to the north, but it had begun to rain, though no more than a light drizzle yet. The sky had become much darker, the sun completely hidden.

Some way from the top of the slope she thought she heard hoofbeats, and stopped to listen. Her heart was pounding so loudly she wondered if she were mistaken. But in another moment she was sure and prayed it might be Paul's horse, not a wild pony. She still had not reached the track when she saw him appear over the ridge.

Her cry was too faint to carry, and he did not hear it. She tried again, but she had so little breath. Desperately she waved her arms above her head.

The horse shied at the sudden movement. Paul reined in and looked down the slope. Then, seeing her, he dismounted and, the reins looped over his arm, started through the heather towards her.

"Miss Conway, what has happened? Are you hurt?"

She waited, regaining her breath, until he reached her. "*I* am not hurt. But I do need your help."

He gave her a searching look. "Do not try to talk until you are more composed. I will lay my coat on this boulder and you must . . ."

"No," she said again, more firmly. "There is no time. I . . ."

"Miss Conway, you are quite distraught," he interrupted her. "I must insist."

"You will insist on nothing," she exclaimed impatiently, and gestured towards the river. "That is where you are wanted, down there in the old tinners' building."

"But no one uses that nowadays. Surely . . ."

"Oh, if you will only listen!" In exasperation she thumped his arm. "Let me explain, *please*."

"Very well," he agreed with reluctance. "But I do not advise you to stand too long in this chill drizzle."

As briefly and clearly as she could, she told him. His face grew grave, then filled with doubt.

"Are you sure this really happened?" he asked. "One hears strange sounds on Dartmoor and imagines all sorts of things."

She clenched her hands and drew a deep breath. "Do you really suppose my imagination would conjure up an escaped prisoner? Dartmoor has many ghosts, I am told. But they are more likely to be devil hounds or headless coachmen than a French boy with a broken leg. I may be merely a woman, Dr. Leland, but I am not completely a fool."

He looked at her a moment longer, then took her arm. "If you will lead me to this boy . . ."

She could not help retorting, "I would have done so five minutes ago had you not persisted in doubting me."

Together they descended the hillside, Paul's arm supporting her, his horse stumbling and slithering down behind them. He tethered the animal to a tree near the ruin, and unfastened his saddlebag.

"I will go in first," Crissa said. "Your appearance may well frighten him." She realised at once that she could have put it more tactfully, but he was still regarding her with an air of disbelief that irritated her, so that she let the remark pass.

Stepping carefully over the stones at the entrance, she called softly, "I have come back, and brought a doctor with me."

There was no answer from the dark interior. Crissa said, over her shoulder, "Perhaps he has fainted. He was in dreadful pain."

Paul had a hand under her arm as they entered. "Where is he? I can see nothing in this gloom."

"Over there," she answered, pointing. "I pulled away some ivy to give more light. But . . ." She went forward a few steps, then stopped, at a loss. "He must have dragged himself into the corner. Monsieur. Monsieur."

Paul said, "Miss Conway, I understood you to say this French youth has a broken leg. People with fractures do not willingly move the injured limb."

"But he must have done," she insisted. "This is exactly where he was lying. That shaft of light between the ivy fell full on his face—here." She knelt and felt cautiously along the ground. Her fingers touched only loose stones and rotting wood.

Paul was standing just inside the entrance. She rose and faced him. "Will you not at least help me to find him? The place is small enough, and he certainly could not have . . ."

"I think there is little point in searching. You are not likely to find him."

"Why not? He could not possibly have gone further, he was so badly injured and weak. Besides, I told him I was going for help and he trusted me, I am sure. He even . . ."

"Yes?" Paul's voice was exasperatingly calm.

"He—he held my hand."

Her eyes had grown more used now to the dimness and she saw that his face was grave. There was something else in his expression too, which she did not understand.

She asked incredulously, "You do not believe me, do you?"

"Oh, yes. That is, I believe you are telling the truth as it seems to you."

"I have not the least notion what that riddle can mean," she retorted angrily. "I told you the truth. I will repeat it. I came down the hillside . . ."

"Why? Why did you come down that rough slope when you were on a perfectly good path?"

"Because I was . . ." She stopped short. She certainly was not going to tell him she had been scared by an old woman whom he considered harmless. "I had my reasons," she ended haughtily.

"Very well. And after you reached the bottom of the hill?"

"I came along the path beside the river. I felt safer there and . . ." At once she realised the slip, and went on hurriedly, "I was passing this place when I heard a cry. I didn't know what it might be and I was a little frightened and began to run. Then I fell and . . ."

"You fell?" His voice was sharp. "Did you hit your head?"

"No, I did not! Really, Dr. Leland, if you are suggesting that my mind is deranged . . ."

"I am suggesting nothing of the kind. Please go on, Miss Conway."

"It was my elbow I hurt. Here, you may see for yourself." She pushed back her cloak and showed him the reddened skin below the short sleeve of her gown.

"That must have given you a nasty jar," he said.

"It did," she agreed with feeling. "I saw stars and I could not help crying out with the pain, and then I was not sure whether it was my own cry I heard or someone else's. Then I recognised the French language and knew there really was someone in trouble, in here."

"And so you came to investigate? That was brave."

"Oh, I armed myself. Look, here is the stick I carried." Triumphantly she brandished it before him.

"And then?" he persisted, sounding not at all impressed.

"Then I saw the boy. He was dressed in rough clothes and as white as a ghost." Again she caught herself up, regretting her choice of words. "And—and I fetched him some water. Why, the mug must be here somewhere. I left it beside him." Again she went on her knees where the French youth had been lying and felt on the ground. There was no mug there. Unsteadily she got to her feet.

"Dr. Leland, I beg you, search this place. I cannot have imagined this. I *cannot*."

"Very well," he said in a tone he would have used to humour a child. "I will do so, if only to convince *you* that there is no one here." Deliberately he brought out his tinder box and a stub of candle from his saddlebag. With her close behind him, he shone the light into every possible recess, behind every fallen slab of granite.

He blew out the candle and said quietly, "Come outside now, Miss Conway. I think the fresh air, and perhaps a little brandy . . ."

Trembling, she allowed him to support her to where his horse was tethered. She took his flask and drank too quickly, coughing and gasping. She looked vaguely up and down the riverside path, shadowy now in the failing light; then back to the derelict shelter. Her fingers shook as she tucked a strand of hair beneath the hood of her cloak.

"I—I do not understand," she said, "What has happened to him—to me? You never did believe me, did you? You were certain from the start we should not find this boy."

He put a hand beneath her elbow, saw her wince, and immediately changed his hold to her other arm. "Yes, I was certain. Because, you see, he had already *been* found."

"What do you mean? I was only gone a matter of twenty minutes or so . . ."

"I do not mean he was found here. But in Tavistock, this morning. Although he had not then a

169

broken leg. But that also can be explained. Your . . ."

"I want *everything* explained," she said sharply.

"Yes, of course, all in good time."

She wrenched herself free. "No. Now. You think I am mad."

"No, no. It is merely that your imagination, under great strain . . ."

"How could my imagination play such tricks?" she demanded fiercely. "I saw this boy. I spoke to him. He told me he was from the depot at Princetown."

"That was true enough. But he and an older man who escaped with him were captured in Tavistock earlier in the day. You must have heard about this, Miss Conway, and dwelt upon it. You went for a walk in a lonely part of the moor, you were frightened though you will not tell me by what. You scrambled down a rough hillside, heard a sound, probably a sheep or a pony, which again frightened you and you began to run. You fell and were badly shaken." He took hold of her hands and began to chafe them. The expression in his eyes was the same as when he looked at Hetty the night her baby was born. "It is nothing to be anxious about, or ashamed. You are overwrought. You have had too much anxiety of late, over your sister, over Armand, and your aunt. When people are overtired and under as much strain as you have endured of late, they can imagine things, have hallucinations. The trouble is usually very soon corrected, with rest and a soothing medicine."

Despite their gentleness, his words frightened her. She did not want to believe what he said. Yet was it not true that her imagination might have been too vivid of late? Her fears for Hetty's child, her suspicions of Aunt Clara, the inexplicable panic she had experienced when that old woman looked at her up there on the lonely track?

Making a last desperate effort to escape the belief that he was right, she demanded, "Dr. Leland, might it not have been you who suffered from a hallucination? Armand has often told me how hard you work, and Mrs. Barlow said you drive yourself to the limits of endurance. Might not *you* have imagined the capture of this French boy?"

He turned a little away and passed a hand across his forehead. "With all my heart I wish I had," he answered heavily. "For he was taken captive in my house."

8

Despite the potion Paul had left for her, Crissa could not sleep. After what seemed hours of trying to lie still so that she would not disturb Hetty, while her dulled mind still sought for a feasible explanation, she could stand it no longer. Slipping quietly from bed, she tiptoed into the little dressing closet where their maid slept. Closing the door carefully behind her, she woke Phoebe, bidding her be quiet. Then she lit a candle and sat on the truckle-bed, pulling the coverlet around her.

"Phoebe, I must talk to you. Are you awake enough to listen?"

"Yes, Miss Clarissa," the maid answered, wide-eyed. "Is it about Miss Henrietta?"

"No. Phoebe, something very strange happened to me today, something I cannot talk about to Hetty for it would worry her, and Aunt Clara must not learn that I went for a walk alone on the moor. If I tell you about it, you are to promise faithfully not to breathe a word to another soul."

"For sure I won't," the girl answered in an awed voice; then wet her finger and crossed her throat. "There, now I've sworn it."

She listened attentively, sitting up in bed with her arms clasped around her knees, a bunch of curls escaping from her linen nightcap, her eyes growing bigger and bigger.

"What do you make of that?" Crissa asked when she had finished her story.

"I can tell you what happened to you, Miss Clarissa," the maid said decisively. " 'Tis simple to my mind, though not something as I like to happen to a mistress of mine."

"What was it, then?"

Proebe took a deep breath and thrust out her chest. "You was bewitched, ma'am."

"Do not be absurd."

The girl bridled. "Very well, miss, if you won't be told. But that's what happened, for sure. You said you felt proper queer after that old crone had looked at you. And you're not the one to be frightened of an *ordinary* old woman, that I do know. She put a spell on you, for certain. I've told 'ee all along she had the power of the evil eye."

Was it possible? However much she might scorn Phoebe's suggestion, Crissa could not but remember her feelings on that lonely track. Why, she had even determined to make the sign of the cross should she encounter the old crone again. But, in the event, she had not dared venture back along the track. Instead, she had fled wildly down the hillside and came upon ... Upon what?

"Phoebe, it is not possible for people to materialise out of space."

" 'Course 'tis," the maid declared. "If you'd been brought up on Dartymoor you'd know that well enough. I've told 'ee about Lady Howard's coach and Dewer and his wish hounds. Then there's white horses and suchlike, and pixies and will-o'-the-wisps that lead you into the bogs. There's houses that's haunted and ..."

"But this French boy was not dead," Crissa pointed out. "At the time I saw—I thought I saw him—he was probably being taken back to Princetown. How can anybody be in two places at the same time?"

"That I can't explain," Phoebe admitted. "But that old witch could, for sure."

Crissa got up and walked the few paces possible in the little room. "Even supposing you are right, why should she do this?"

"To do you harm, of course. To make you think, and others too, seemingly, that you'm ... well not quite right in the head. Witches are terrible malicious creatures and she'd bear a grudge against you as well as me for what happened in the churchyard."

Crissa stared at the maid in silence. Then she flung herself on the bed so that it creaked ominously under the combined weight.

"Oh, Phoebe, I do not know what to think. It is all beyond my comprehension." She buried her face in her hands. "As if I have not enough already to weigh down my spirits."

"There, there, ma'am, don't 'ee take on so," the maid urged. "Go back to bed and try to sleep. I'll tell you what I'd do if I was you. I'd go and see the rector and tell him all about it. Some parsons have great power against the witches. This one may have. 'Tis worth a try. And you'd best not go out without me, Miss Clarissa." The maid sighed prodigiously. "Though how I'm to look after you and Miss Henrietta and the baby, I *don't* know."

In the morning, however, there was little chance for Crissa to go out at all. Martha was in a particularly disgruntled mood so that Crissa did more than her usual share of tasks. Aunt Clara had mislaid her spectacles and set her niece to turning the bedroom upside down to hunt for them. When they were found, the old lady clamped them on her nose and fixed Crissa with a penetrating stare.

"What is the matter with you, miss?" she demanded. "You look as if you are sickening for something."

"I am quite well, ma'am, I assure you. I did not sleep well, that is all."

"Why not? Ah, I can guess. Your mind is full of young Monsieur de Beauvoir, I'll be bound."

"I am naturally disturbed on his account."

Aunt Clara sniffed. "It had better go no further than that. For your father would never agree to your marrying a Frenchman, you may be sure."

"Even if I contemplated such a step, Aunt Clara, I should not dream of confronting Papa with that

174

request until Hetty's affairs have been settled. I can wait to decide my future. She cannot."

"Has the post arrived?" her aunt asked.

"Yes."

"And there is still no reply from your father?"

Crissa shook her head. "He must be away from home, probably travelling around as he does quite often to settle some legal matter."

The old lady twitched at her skirt. "Bring the child to me. I have not seen it for two days and I wish to know how it does."

She studied the baby critically, pulling back the shawl from his face. "He is a Conway," she announced with satisfaction. "There is no doubt of it. He looks exactly like Thomas did when he was that age."

It was difficult for Crissa to imagine her father ever having been a baby, let alone resembling this little creature with its dark wisps of hair and tiny mouth. She could not think the child beautiful, as Hetty did, nor as yet feel any pride in being his aunt. But as his fingers curled around hers she felt more pleasure than she would have believed possible and he aroused in her a fierce protectiveness.

She asked doubtfully, "Do you suppose Papa would believe that if you told him so?"

"He can scarcely deny it," Aunt Clara remarked tartly. She took off her spectacles and began to polish them. "Men do not really care for babies, Clarissa, especially as young as this one. Thomas would find it very irksome to have one in the house."

"I did not suppose, ma'am, that we even dared to consider the possibility."

The polishing was continued with increased concentration. "That is quite correct. There are other propositions, however, which might be put to him."

"Such as . . . ?" Crissa prompted when her aunt remained silent.

But the old lady had said as much as she intended. She put on her spectacles again and glared at her niece.

"Why are you standing there doing nothing, miss? I do not encourage idleness in this house, as you know well enough. It vexes me greatly that I myself am forced to practise it at present."

Hetty was sitting at the window when Crissa returned with the baby. Crissa was half-way across the room when her sister cried out.

"Oh, come and look! Whatever is happening?"

Crissa ran to the window. Between the trees in the drive appeared a carriage, crammed with young men, all shouting and singing and waving. They leaned from the windows. One clung to the roof, another was riding the lead horse. Yet another hung on behind.

"Who are they?" Hetty asked. "And what are they doing here?"

Swiftly Crissa handed her the baby. "They are French officers," she answered, her voice shaking with excitement. "And they are bringing Armand home."

She reached the hall so quickly that she had the door open before the carriage pulled up. She ran forward, hands outstretched, modesty and decorum completely forgotten.

"Armand. Armand. Oh, how good it is to see you! And you are free!"

Laughing, he extricated himself from his friends

and jumped from the vehicle. He kissed her hands and looked as if he would have kissed her cheek also. But, recovering herself, she drew back. His compatriots crowded round, chattering gaily in a mixture of French and English. She caught some of their remarks.

"Lucky Armand. Worth being in prison. Who told us that English girls are cold? *Elle est si belle, si belle. I* would break my parole for this one, *certainement.*"

Armand turned to them. "I am obliged to you, *mes amis,* for your escort. Unfortunately, though I am sure Mademoiselle Clarissa would be delighted to invite you inside to celebrate my release, this is not her house and it is impossible."

"*Quel dommage!*" they exclaimed. "What a disappointment! It is because of *le dragon, naturellement.*"

One, older than the others, stepped forward and bowed to her. "We understand, mademoiselle," he said in perfect English. "We will leave you in peace now to talk to Armand." Unmistakeably his eyes suggested what she and Armand would talk about. Then he became very serious. "But first I wish to speak for all of us here, and others of our compatriots who would wish to be here. There is not one amongst us, mademoiselle, who does not appreciate your action in going immediately to the depot at Princetown and trying your best to get Lieutenant de Beauvoir freed. You and Dr. Leland are indeed our friends. And we do need friends, mademoiselle. We may appear gay on the surface. But underneath, here"—he touched his chest—"there is

177

often much sadness. You will allow us to make you a little gift?"

He drew from the pocket of his coat a small package. Glancing enquiringly at Armand, Crissa took it hesitantly; then, as she saw the circle of expectant eyes upon her, opened it carefully. It contained the model of a schooner and was so fragile and delicately carved she thought at first it was fashioned from ivory.

"It is beautiful!" she exclaimed. "How very kind of you all. I shall treasure it greatly."

"It was carved by a prisoner at Princetown," the officer told her. "From meat bones."

She turned it over, examining every facet of the exquisite work. Then, unexpectedly, she could not see it properly, for her eyes were misted with tears.

Armand looked closely at her. "You must not cry, Crissa. This is a happy day, not one for tears."

"I—I am so touched.

The young men looked puzzled. Rapidly Armand translated for them. Crissa held out her hand.

"I have never had a nicer present, Monsieur le Capitaine. My heartfelt thanks to you all."

They cheered her, tossing their hats in the air; then scrambled back into the carriage and started off down the drive, singing at the tops of their voices. When they had disappeared, Armand turned to Crissa.

"I am sorry if it upset you. But they insisted. Will *le dragon* be very cross?"

"She may not have heard. Her room is at the back, you remember. She still must keep to it, on Dr. Leland's orders."

"I would think that everyone on Dartmoor must

hear them," he said, laughing. Then his expression changed. "Is that your sister at the window?"

Crissa glanced up. "Yes. She is waving to you, I think."

As he looked up, his face had the eagerness of a boy's. He raised his hat in salute and made Hetty a profound bow. His eyes were bright as he turned to Crissa. "So we are to be friends? Oh, that is good!"

As they went together into the drawing-room, Crissa looked at him more closely. His features seemed finger drawn and he was rather pale. His right arm now was free of the sling.

"So Captain d'Aubois has recovered?"

"Yes." Armand shrugged. "I suppose I should be glad, since I am free, and back again with you, *ma chère* Crissa. I, too, have brought you a present, though it is not as fine as that one." He smiled ruefully. "It proves expensive in prison for a man who wishes to keep up some semblance of being a gentleman. And I brought back one for *la petite* Hetty too, for her *bébé*. Do you think she will like it?" He held up a tiny doll made of gaily coloured plaited straw. "They are not supposed to make these because it takes trade away from the country people. But they do, of course, and sell them to get more food, or money to gamble with."

"It is delightful," Crissa said warmly. "I am quite sure Hetty will think so, too. And little Peter when he is old enough to play with it."

"And this is for you." He put into her hands a ring stand made of polished wood, dark inlaid with light.

"How charming!" she exclaimed with pleasure.

"Armand, it is most generous of you. But you should not have . . ."

"Why not? I like buying *cadeaux*. And for whom else should I buy them? I have no family in England. No fiancée. It is natural, then, that I make you a gift, since you have been so kind. I have kept all your letters and your sister's. I thought of you every day. Sit down beside me and let me look at you. It has seemed so long."

She felt the colour rising to her cheeks, the quickened beat of her heart. "It is not so very long, Armand. Less than two weeks, in fact."

"It has seemed a lifetime. But it was my own fault that it was no more than a day. If I had not fought that duel . . ." He shrugged. His face became serious. "If I had not been an officer on my parole of honour, but an ordinary sailor sent to a prison like that one, I would have done everything in my power to escape. Like those poor devils who were brought back yesterday."

"Yes, I heard about them. One was captured at Dr. Leland's house. Did you know that?"

"Yes, I knew," Armand said regretfully. "I hope it will not be bad for him. That was the boy who gave the soldiers the slip, though I do not think they want it to be known."

"What do you mean, Armand? Gave the soldiers the slip?"

"The story does no credit to your English militiamen and I think they want to keep it dark. But we heard it—in there. He was a drummer boy, the one taken at Paul's house, and he was being marched back to Princetown when somehow he managed to divert the soldiers' attention and run off. He disappeared into some trees, it seems, beside the river. The water made so much noise the soldiers could not tell where he was, and they were hampered with their boots and their accoutrement." He glanced at her in alarm. "Why, Crissa, what is the matter? Am I distressing you?"

She put down the presents and clasped her hands tightly together. "No," she said faintly. "Please go on, Armand."

"It is that you have a soft heart, *n'est-ce pas?*" He took her hand and stroked it gently. "It seems the boy made good his escape. But later he was found, in a sort of cave beside the river. He had broken his leg."

She had never really noticed the pattern on the carpet before. Now, after a few minutes, she knew every line and colour. At last she asked, "Did you hear how the soldiers came to know where he was?"

"It was not very clear. An old woman, I think, told them. Crissa, what is it? Oh, *chérie*, I did not mean to upset you."

She rose a little unsteadily. "Forgive me, Armand. I will talk to you later. I am a—a little indisposed this morning, and the excitement of your return . . ."

There was concern in his eyes. "I am sorry. Is there something I can do?"

She shook her head. "No. No, thank you. You have, in fact, done a great deal for me, unknowingly." Gently she disengaged her hand and picked up the gifts. Handing him the straw doll, she managed a smile. "You must give this to Hetty yourself when she is able to come downstairs. And, Armand, I think you should go up now and see Aunt

Clara. She will, I am sure, be as happy as I am at your return."

Paul stood by the drawing-room window, hands clasped beneath his coat tails. His shoulders sagged, his head was bowed.

Crissa paused in the doorway. "You wished to see me, Phoebe said. Did you find Hetty not so well?"

He swung round and came swiftly towards her. "It has nothing to do with your sister. I—I scarcely know how to begin."

"If it is connected with the escaped prisoner," she said coolly, sitting down on the sofa, "you have no need to explain. I have already heard the story from Armand."

He stood before her, smoothing the sleeve of his blue coat in an oddly nervous manner. "Then what am I to say to you? The—the aspect I put upon your story must have caused you hours of anxiety."

"Yes," she agreed in the same detached tone. "You suggested I was overwrought and suffering from hallucinations. Phoebe took the view that I was bewitched. In truth, I found it difficult to decide which was the more distressing version."

Nothing in her previous meetings with him prepared her for his behaviour now. He went on one knee beside her, made as if to take her hand, then swiftly withdrew his own. His expression was that of an uncertain child.

"I acted with the utmost folly," he said, and Crissa was instinctively aware how difficult such an admission was for him. "If I had searched more closely . . . There must have been footprints, signs of the soldiers having been there. Instead, I came immediately to a false conclusion and thereby added to the burden of worries which was already more than you should have borne alone. I have no words, save the most simple ones. I am deeply sorry."

There had been a time, only a few weeks ago, when she would have felt a sense of triumph to see him like this, kneeling beside her, dark head bowed, at her mercy. Now, she took not the slightest pleasure in the sight. On the contrary, she felt a strong desire to stretch out her hand and smooth his hair and tell him that everything was all right, that everyone made mistakes.

She gripped her fingers tightly together and sat a little further back. She said quietly, "I cannot think that you owe me so great an apology. The conclusion you drew yesterday was, after all, a natural one."

"But I put doubt into your mind. I even accused you of lying, I believe."

She shook her head. "No, never that. You were most careful to assure me that you believed I was telling the truth as I saw it." Seeing that he was still dejected, she deliberately lightened her tone. "No great harm has been done, I assure you. The time was very short in which I thought I might be considered a fit case for Bedlam."

"You can laugh about it?" he asked, raising his eyes at last. "You are generous, Miss Conway, as well as courageous. I never met a woman so . . ." He stopped abruptly and rose to his feet. "But Armand is the one to pay compliments. He is so much better at it than I."

"Doubtless he has had more practice. I would consider a compliment from you, Dr. Leland, as— as bearing more weight. Will you not finish your sentence?"

"No." His answer was curt to the point of rudeness. "That is, not now. I have no right at present, not when I am under threat of arrest."

She was on her feet in an instant. "Surely not! You had no part in this prisoner's escape, or so I understood from you yesterday. Why, you were not even there when he was taken."

"That fact has little bearing on the matter. I have been told by Mr. Creber that there was a paper in the boy's pocket with my name and address upon it, together with those of some well-known escape agents who, he hoped, would take him to the coast."

"What folly to carry such evidence on him! But, then, he was only a boy." And she recalled how he had lain there in the semi-darkness saying so hopelessly, "I am not good at being *fugitif*."

She remembered something else, too; the fact that she had been ready to enlist Paul's help, not only to attend to the boy's injury but to hide him if possible, without a thought of the consequences to herself, or to Paul.

She asked anxiously, "They cannot arrest you on such slight evidence, surely?"

"It is not as slight as all that, Miss Conway. I am well known to be sympathetic towards the French prisoners. In the mind of a man like Creber, it is only one step further to help them to escape. Though, to be sure, this is not really his affair for he is only responsible for the parole officers. But, naturally, the Governor at Princetown will listen to him."

"But would they not have arrested you at once if they had been really suspicious?"

"Had not my services been so greatly in demand I think they would have done so. As it is, I feel that Creber has his spies out watching my every move. It would give him great pleasure to see me transported, I believe."

She said, in horror, "They could not do that, surely?"

"Do not look so anxious, Miss Clarissa. To merit such a severe punishment I think they would need to prove a felonious intent, and the motive of monetary gain. And no one, not even Creber, could accuse me of helping French prisoners for money."

"Why should this man want to have you arrested? I noticed the way he looked at you on the night of the concert. There was a—a kind of hatred in his eyes."

Paul turned away. "It is a long story. He has cause."

Once again she could see by his face that he had no intention of telling her more.

"I would not have blamed you if you *had* helped that boy," she said. "I cannot get the thought out of my head that he will believe I betrayed him. I told him I was going to fetch a doctor. Instead, the soldiers came. He must think I sent them. When, in fact, it was that old woman who Phoebe is so sure is a black witch. I wish she *had* been stoned that day in the churchyard."

"Because she seized the chance of some extra money?"

"I do not understand you."

He spoke in the patient voice she had come to know so well. "That old woman lives in a hovel out on the moor—oh yes, with the traditional black cat. She feeds on anything she may pick up or gather from the hedgerows and fields, or, if she is lucky, on the offerings laid at her door by those who fear and wish to placate her. So you can see what a reward of five pounds must mean to her. She is, of course, deranged in her mind. But she is to be pitied for that, not cursed."

"And it was she who led the soldiers to your house in the first place?"

"I do not know. It may have been. Creber, more likely."

"Yet you do not blame either of them?"

"Who am I to judge my fellows? I have been weak enough myself in the past. And *my* weakness cost a life, and much sorrow."

Crissa waited, while he stood staring out of the window, apparently deep in thought.

"Yet you were prepared to judge Hetty and me, that first day," she said when he did not speak.

He swung round to face her. "Yes, and so wrongly. I saw you then as two fashionably dressed young women, sitting comfortably in your carriage and thinking only of the inconvenience to yourselves, and heartlessly refusing to move so that I could reach those unfortunate men. I judged *you* to be like—like Miriam. I was never more mistaken in my life. For you are . . ." He broke off and glanced out of the window. "There is a carriage coming up the drive. You are expecting visitors?"

"Why, no." She joined him at the window, disappointed by the interruption. For she believed that at last she was about to hear what had happened in the past to make him suspicious of women and turn him against marriage.

The horses were just emerging from the trees. She stared at them, and at the heavy vehicle they drew, and caught her breath.

Paul asked, "What is the matter? You have turned quite pale."

"It is—our carriage," she whispered. "It must surely have been sent to take us home. But—like this, without any warning?"

"There is someone inside," Paul said, his height giving him a better view. "A gentleman dressed in black and wearing a wig, I think."

She pressed close to the pane, then drew back. "It is Papa!" she exclaimed in dismay. "Oh, poor Hetty!"

"*Poor* Hetty?" Paul repeated in surprise. "Surely your father will be very proud to have a grandson? Admittedly the child is small as yet, but he will grow."

"You do not understand," she said hopelessly. "I have not told you everything. And now I do not know in the least what to do for the best."

His hand was beneath her elbow. "Suppose you tell me now, quickly, before he enters? For may there not be some way in which I can help?"

She looked at him dully, finding it difficult to think clearly. So much had happened, and she had had so little sleep last night. The pressure of his fingers and the compulsion in his eyes jerked her into rapid explanation.

"It is true that Hetty is married now, but she

was not when . . . Peter married her as soon as he knew about the baby. Papa was away and they married in secret, because Papa did not approve of Peter, you see. He was a young naval officer without any money and not of a suitable background in Papa's opinion. And when Papa learned from me all that had happened, and that Peter had been killed, he would not even see Hetty, but sent us both here to Aunt Clara, so that Hetty should have the baby in secret and return to Dartmouth . . ." She stopped as she heard the front door bell clang loudly.

"Yes?" Paul prompted urgently. "To return to Dartmouth . . . ?"

"Without her baby. She was to forget Peter, forget her marriage and her child."

"But that is monstrous!" he exclaimed, and even in that moment of crisis Crissa realised he had used her own words. "It cannot be allowed."

She heard Martha go grumbling across the hall, her startled exclamation as she recognised the visitor. She heard her father's voice, dry, precise, so like Aunt Clara's. And she knew her courage was at an end. Against the man who stood stiffly in the hall, handing Martha his hat and gloves and silver-topped cane, all her defiant words would be useless. If Hetty herself could not move him to pity, then there was nothing she could do. She knew it in that moment with a terrible, hopeless certainty.

She saw Martha gesture towards the drawing-room. In another moment her father was standing in the doorway, greeting her briefly, glancing with curiosity at Paul.

"I appear to be interrupting a tête-à-tête," he remarked drily. "Clarissa, present me to your friend."

"This is Dr. Leland, sir," she said, making him a formal curtsey. "He has been attending Hetty and Aunt Clara."

Her father's eyebrows were slightly raised. "You are somewhat younger than I expected, sir. Your skill would appear to outrun your years, for Clarissa informed me that you saved my daughter's life in what might be considered very dangerous circumstances."

Paul bowed. "You are very kind to say so, sir."

"And how is Henrietta? Sit down, Clarissa, and do not hover in that irritating manner." As Paul pushed forward a chair, he shook his head. "I have been sitting overlong in that jolting carriage. The roads in these parts seem little better than when I was a boy."

"Mrs. Stanhope is gaining a little more strength each day," Paul said. "But she is still very weak, Mr. Conway, and tires easily. Naturally, her child is a great comfort to her in her tragic position."

Crissa held her breath. Her father's face was expressionless.

"Quite so." He took out a small silver box and flicked open the lid. "Do you take snuff, sir?"

"Thank you, no. Mr. Conway, I think you were not expected?"

"That is correct." He took a pinch of snuff, drew out a large linen handkerchief, and sneezed. "Clarissa's letter reached me eventually at Plymouth where I had certain affairs to settle. Finding myself with some free time, I decided to come in person rather than reply by post."

Crissa felt the usual irritation at her father's

words and manner. If only he were a different man, one who would say, "I could not wait to see my daughter and my grandson." But it was useless regretting.

She asked, "Does that mean, then, that you have not come to take us home, Papa?"

Before her father could answer, Paul stepped forward. "I should most strongly advise against it. Mrs. Stanhope is certainly in no fit state to travel any distance yet and the baby, being premature, should not be exposed to the chill air."

Crissa stared down at her clasped hands. She dared not look at her father.

"Quite so," he said again, non-committally. "I assume, however, that you are not going to suggest that my sudden and unexpected arrival will have any deleterious effect upon my daughter?"

Paul said equably, "I see no reason why it should, sir. After all, Mrs. Stanhope is devoted to you. She has often spoken of you to me and always with the greatest admiration. And although it is natural she would have wished the child to bear some resemblance to its father, she contents herself that it should bear your stamp instead."

"*My stamp?*" Thomas Conway echoed incredulously.

"Oh, yes, Papa," Crissa confirmed hurriedly. "Aunt Clara is quite certain of it."

"Indeed?" He snapped-to the lid of his snuff-box and tucked away his handkerchief. "Then I had better take a look, though I do not expect to be flattered by the likeness."

Crissa rose to her feet. "I think I had better go and warn Hetty, Papa."

He turned at the door. "Why should you suppose she needs warning, Clarissa? Unless you have been poisoning her mind against me."

Crissa's control snapped. "Papa! I have done no such thing! I have not even told Hetty that you planned for her child to be taken from her. I warn you, Papa, if you insist on that monstrous cruelty, you will have only yourself to blame if you not only lose Hetty's affection, but endanger her very life. For you will break her heart."

He regarded her in silence, then turned to Paul. "You are probably by now quite used to my daughter's extravagant expressions. As a man of medicine, a profession calling for as much precision of language as the law, you doubtless deplore them as much as I do."

Crissa saw Paul's mouth tighten, the familiar hard look come into his eyes. He faced Thomas Conway squarely and spoke with slow emphasis.

"Sometimes, I admit, sir, Miss Conway is a little impulsive in her choice of words. But in what she has just said about her sister, I concur completely. At the time of Mrs. Stanhope's confinement, I knew only too well that if I could not save her child, I should be unable to save her, either. Because, you see, she would have lost all will to live. That situation, Mr. Conway, has not altered in the least degree."

Two patches of red appeared on the lawyer's cheeks. He pinched in his nostrils in the action so familiar in his sister. Then abruptly he turned on his heel and went from the room and up the stairs.

Crissa said, in an awed voice, "I never heard anyone speak to my father like that. Is it possible that you have achieved in two minutes what I could not manage with all my imploring or defiance?"

"I hope so," Paul said. "For if he does not heed my warning, he is like to find himself a murderer."

"What do you mean?" she asked in alarm.

"Did you not think I meant what I said? You were perfectly right in declaring that to take her child away from your sister would break her heart, I would not answer for the consequences. In time, perhaps, she may overcome her grief and marry again and bear other children. But for the present, there is only her son—and the comfort you give by your constant devotion."

"I take no credit for that," she said, although she felt warmed by his praise. "It is easy enough to care devotedly for someone one loves. I find it a great deal more difficult to be kind to Aunt Clara."

"That does not surprise me. And Armand? Is it easy to be kind to Armand?"

"Why, of course."

"Because you love him?"

She gasped at the directness of his question. She framed her answer carefully. "I find him attractive and charming and excellent company. But as to love . . . I think I am only just beginning to learn the meaning of that word."

Because of you, she added to herself, realising it with a sense of shock. Because of the way you knelt before me just now and humbled yourself when you thought you had distressed me. Because of the way you understood so immediately about Hetty and have tried to help her. Because of your obstinacy and your arrogance and your gentleness and compassion. Because of the way your hair grows, and your sudden smile that makes you look so much younger, and the skill in your hands, and your voice . . . Because of a thousand things I doubt I will ever be able to tell you, you are so set upon your single state.

"There is someone else you care for, then?" he persisted. "At Dartmouth, perhaps?"

"There is no one of the least importance to me at Dartmouth. Though why you should question me like this . . ."

"It is impertinent of me, I agree." He picked up hat and whip. "I must be on my rounds. And show my face in Tavistock before long, or they will think I have broken *my* parole and vanished."

She went with him to the door. "You did not tell me what *is* likely to happen to you if you are arrested."

"As I said, I scarcely think I shall be sent to the plantations," he answered lightly. "At the least it will mean a fine. At worst, a term in gaol."

"*Oh, no!*"

He looked surprised at her cry of dismay.

"But you have done nothing wrong," she protested. "They cannot imprison you simply for being kind to the French prisoners."

"If they should do so, would you rush to my rescue as you did to Armand's?"

She could not look at him. Her answer was barely audible. "I should find a way."

"Yes," he said softly, "I believe you would. You are a great righter of wrongs, Miss Clarissa. I see a great deal of your aunt in your character." As she started to protest, he added hastily, "That was intended as a compliment, though you may not consider it so. It is not only because you have your mother's looks that Miss Conway opposes you. It is also because she recognises a will as strong as her own. And at her age she has no intention of coming off second best to a girl of twenty-one." Untethering his horse, he said over his shoulder, "I will come to see your sister tomorrow, unless she has need of me before. Or unless I am in gaol."

He was smiling as he mounted and rode away. But Crissa had caught the note of anxiety in his voice and seen that the smile was not in his eyes.

Armand was free. Hetty's fate was being decided at this moment in the bedroom above. But she herself had yet another worry on her mind. And she had not the least notion how she might help the man who had awakened in her heart the love she had been seeking in a succession of admirers. She knew now what her mother had meant when she spoke of truly loving a man. She knew what Hetty had felt for Peter. For if Paul Leland should be sent to gaol—or if he should stay free and not return her love—then life, despite all the Armands and Harrys in the world, would be desolate indeed.

9

Crissa could scarcely believe her ears. In Aunt Clara's bedroom an argument was taking place, and neither the old lady nor her brother appeared to have heard Crissa's knock or to be aware that she stood hesitating in the doorway.

"The matter is settled, Clara," Thomas Conway declared, rising from his seat in the window embrasure.

His sister's voice was equally forceful. "But, Thomas, I am perfectly willing for them to stay with me at least until the weather worsens. Dr. Leland, I am sure, would agree that it is better for Henrietta to be completely rested before she undertakes the journey to Dartmouth, and that the child should be given every chance to grow strong before facing the risk of being taken outdoors."

"He can come to no harm if he is well wrapped up."

"But you yourself have complained about the state of the roads. Supposing a horse should go lame, or"—there was a note of triumph in Aunt Clara's voice—"or a wheel come off the carriage. In that case, both Henrietta and the child would be exposed to the . . ."

"That is all the more reason for their leaving before the weather does become bad," her brother capped her argument. "I would have thought, in your present state of ill-health, that you would be only too thankful to be rid of the responsibility."

The old lady drew herself up. "I am not in ill-health. It is merely a trifling and temporary indisposition. As for responsibility, I have accepted that all my life, as you should know."

"Yes, that is true," he acknowledged. "You made self-sacrifices for me in the past and have done so again now. I am not ungrateful to you, Clara."

"I have merely done my duty."

Crissa cleared her throat. Her father turned,

frowning. "Clarissa, how long have you been standing there, eavesdropping?"

"I had no intention of eavesdropping, sir," she protested. "I came with a message from Martha. She wishes to have your orders for the day, ma'am."

"I have written them here," Aunt Clara said. But when Crissa would have taken the paper from her, she kept hold of it, and spoke to her brother.

"I did not like your wife, Thomas, and I do not like your daughter—not this one. But I trust I am a fair-minded woman and I wish to give praise where it is due. Clarissa, for all her defiant ways, has proved during these difficult weeks both willing and capable. Moreover, although I confess to being alarmed at the prospect of having her under my roof at the same time as Lieutenant de Beauvoir, especially when I myself was confined to my bedroom, I have no reason to suppose she has taken advantage of the situation. In fact, the lady who has been kind enough to act as chaperone to her, has reported Clarissa's behaviour as entirely proper."

"I am gratified to hear it," her brother said drily. "After much heart searching I have found it possible to be reconciled to Hetty. But any misconduct on Clarissa's part I should have considered quite unpardonable. I will leave you now to discuss your domestic arrangements."

When he had gone, Crissa said, "It was indeed kind of you, Aunt Clara, to speak on my behalf." As she took the proffered paper, she impulsively held the old lady's thin hand between her own. "I —I wish . . ."

Aunt Clara did not immediately withdraw her

hand. But there was no warmth in her eyes. "No, Clarissa. You and I will never like each other. But dislike, as you will learn, does not preclude respect and admiration."

Crissa went from her aunt's room, feeling both elated and depressed. Aunt Clara's character, like her father's, was so foreign to her own that she found both of them impossible to understand. Not that it mattered. What was important was that Hetty was restored to favour and would be allowed to keep her child.

Half-way down the stairs Crissa paused. On the sofa in the drawing-room lay Hetty, looking pale but pretty, a wrap over her knees, the baby in his cradle on the floor beside her. The cradle was being rocked by a foot encased in an elegant black boot with a turned-down cuff of yellow leather. Armand was talking animatedly, while Hetty interposed a quiet remark now and then, and was even smiling at him.

Crissa recalled Paul's words. "One day your sister will overcome her grief and marry again." She remembered Hetty telling her how she would dearly like a husband who would oblige her in all things. And Armand was the most obliging of men. Armand—and Hetty? A foolish notion, no doubt. Yet the war would not last for ever, and they were a deal more suited to each other than she and Armand.

She went on down the stairs, deep in thought. Everything had turned out so much better than she expected. Her anxieties on Hetty's behalf, and on Armand's, were ended. She should be feeling carefree now, eagerly looking forward to going home and taking up again the familiar, pleasant life she had known before Hetty's indiscretion had put an end to it for them both. But there was no joy in that prospect now. The future held no hope of happiness if Paul Leland should have no part in it.

What had happened to him? Was he still free, or had he in fact been arrested? If he had, what could she do to help him? She had told him she would find a way. Yet, how was it possible? She could no more set herself against the law than she could break down the rules and regulations of the Transport Board on Armand's behalf.

Through the kitchen window she saw her father walking in the garden. And suddenly she realised there was a way to help Paul. Thrusting Aunt Clara's list into Martha's hand, she rushed outside, and almost collided with her father in her haste.

"Papa, may I speak to you, please?" she entreated breathlessly. "It is about Dr. Leland and very important. Papa, will you listen to me, *please?*"

Half an hour later she set off for Tavistock with her usual springy step, all her senses alive to the bright morning. Despite the sun, the wind blowing off the moor was keen, and she had put on her fur-trimmed green pelisse and matching bonnet and carried her muff. On the turnpike road she met two French officers taking their morning walk. They turned smartly at the milestone and ranged themselves on either side of her.

"You will permit us to accompany you, mademoiselle?"

She was gratified by their admiring glances, by their eagerness for her company. But if she had been in any need of a proof of her changed feelings, this encounter provided it. The Frenchmen were young. They were handsome. They were charming and agreeable and complimentary. But they were not Paul. When she parted with their company at the gate of Mrs. Barlow's house, they were banished immediately from her mind.

She met Mrs. Barlow in the drive. "Were you coming to call on me, my dear? How very nice. But I have to go into Tavistock. Will you walk there with me?"

"I shall be glad to," Crissa answered eagerly. "I have such good news to give you, ma'am."

The older woman listened attentively as Crissa told her about their father's arrival and his changed attitude.

"That *is* good news. And Armand is back, I hear. So now your worries are at an end? But it is not so fortunate for me, Crissa dear. For it means I shall lose your company. How soon will you be leaving?"

"As soon as Hetty is strong enough to travel. Papa wishes us to return with him, but it depends on Dr. Leland. You have heard he is under suspicion?"

"I have, indeed, and I am told all Tavistock is up in arms about it. Even if it should be true that he helped a prisoner to escape, I do not envy anyone trying to convict him. He is so well thought of, and so needed here."

"I have been speaking to my father. He has expressed himself perfectly willing to defend Dr. Leland should he be arrested. Papa is a very clever lawyer, Mrs. Barlow, and he is grateful to Paul— Dr. Leland for saving Hetty."

"Why, that is splendid! But perhaps it will not come to a court case."

"I hope not. But I thought . . ." Crissa twisted her fingers together inside her muff. "I thought, while we are in Tavistock, I might perhaps call and tell Dr. Leland about Papa's offer, or leave a note should he not be at home."

"Does he not visit Grimstone House each day?"

"Yes, but sometimes not until later. I would like him to know as soon as possible." She felt her companion's eyes upon her. "After all," she added with what she hoped sounded convincing reasonableness, "my family has cause to be very grateful to him." Then, carefully casual, she said, "When we were on our way to Princetown, you started to tell me why Dr. Leland had never married. It seems a great pity that a man so admired, and who devotes himself so much to other people, should not have a wife and family to give him some comfort at home."

Again she was aware of her friend's sidelong glance. Mrs. Barlow walked a few yards in silence, then she appeared to make up her mind.

"Very well, my dear, I will tell you. Though I do not suppose Dr. Leland likes the story bruited about, it is known well enough in this district. Some years ago he formed an attachment to the daughter of a local landowner. Those of us who knew what a selfish, spoiled young woman she was, deplored his choice. But he was young and apparently so infatuated that he was blind to the fact that she would make a most unsuitable wife for a man in his position. We had then, as now, a great number of French officers in the town and some of them, as you will have seen for yourself, are not short of money. Miriam's father kept open house for them, and it was very gay with dances and supper parties in the summer and musical tea parties in the winter. The Frenchmen, as you know, have too much time on their hands. Paul, as a young doctor starting his practice here, had little money or time to spare. Naturally I do not know what actually passed between them, but I should imagine that Miriam taunted him with preferring his patients' company to hers."

"That was foolish," Crissa could not help interrupting. "He is a doctor. His patients must come first."

This time her companion's look was direct and thoughtful. "You are quite right, my dear. But, as I told you, this young woman's sole thought was for her own pleasure. One day Dr. Leland was at her home when a call came for him to visit a patient at a remote farm on the moor. It so happened that it was after curfew time for the Frenchmen and for once Dr. Leland had Miriam to himself. I am not usually given to listening to gossip, but the tale goes that she issued an ultimatum; either he stay with her an hour longer, or not see her again. He remained. When he reached the farm, it was too late. Instead of an old man dying a natural death, to whom he had expected to be called, he found the farmer's daughter, who was staying in the house, terribly burned and beyond his help. The woman's husband never forgave him, and Paul has never forgiven himself. Ever since, he has not spared himself. He is a man plagued by his conscience and holding to the belief that love for a woman can

201

lead only to weakness and temptation and the forsaking of his duty."

"Does he *really* believe all women to be like that? Indeed, he must be blind to the many marriages in which devoted wives helped their husbands, not harmed them. What happened to this girl?"

"She married the son of a baronet and went to live in London where doubtless she is able to live the life of entertainment she craved."

Crissa was thoughtful as they came within sight of Abbey Bridge. On the seat beside the river, Armand had introduced her to Paul and she had thought him the most churlish and disagreeable of men. Now she understood. For he had thought her at that time another Miriam. And now? Surely now he thought differently, if his words of yesterday were of any significance? If *this* was his only reason for turning his back upon marriage, all she had to overcome was prejudice. It was not so hopeless, after all.

She smiled at her companion. "Gentlemen are sometimes very foolish, are they not, ma'am?"

"Oh yes, very," Mrs. Barlow agreed gravely, but there was a hint of amusement in her eyes. "And, as you will doubtless have learned by now, Crissa, it rests with the women who love them to show where they are wrong."

Crissa stopped and gazed at the older woman in astonishment. "You—you have guessed?"

Mrs. Barlow took her arm. "My dear, you are an open book to those who are fond of you, I think. Indeed I wish that you might win him, for I can think of no more suitable wife for Paul. And he is in great need of one."

Crissa's cheeks were burning. "There is so little time, though, and I would not like you to think that I would . . ."

"Throw yourself at his head? I know you better than that. We are nearly at his house. Do you wish me to come with you?"

"Oh, indeed, yes. Papa would not at all approve of my calling alone upon Dr. Leland. Why are you laughing?"

"Because, child, you are at one moment so proud and rebellious, and the next you assume the appearance of the most dutiful of daughters, the most decorous of young ladies."

"Armand told me the same thing, so I suppose it must be true."

"There is no need to look. as if I have reprimanded you. I find it a wholly delightful mixture. And if Paul Leland does not think likewise, he will be extremely foolish."

Crissa was curious to see inside Paul's house, which stood close to the church. There was a group of people before the gate: two French officers, some women she assumed were shopkeepers' wives, and Mr. Creber, the prisoners' agent.

As Mrs. Barlow lifted the latch, one of the women said, "You'll not find the doctor at home."

"Our business is not urgent," the widow replied. "We can leave a message."

"There be no knowing when he'll receive it," the woman said with a sniff.

Crissa caught her breath. "Do you mean he has been taken into custody?"

"No, nor likely to be, it seems. Mr. Creber here, though he don't like the job, I'm thinking, has come to tell the doctor so. They've no real case against him, as we all know well enough."

Another woman, who looked like a farmer's wife, stepped forward. Her eyes were alight with the pleasure of imparting news. "He'm gone, the doctor. And nobody knows where he be tu."

"Surely he has simply gone on his rounds?" Mrs. Barlow suggested.

"Since yesterday afternoon? The last that was seen of him was at Magpie Farm about six o'clock last evening. He've not been home since, nor nobody had a sight of un."

The prisoners' agent said sarcastically, "Perhaps you were all too sure of Dr. Leland's innocence. His disappearance may be because he had cause to believe he *would* be arrested."

One of the Frenchmen pushed forward. "You are determined to make him a criminal. It is not so. He is a good man and loyal to his country. He likes us, but he does not break the law."

"And how would *you* know, monsieur?" Mr. Creber demanded arrogantly.

"I know it—here." The young man patted the left side of his chest.

"Then why has he run away? Does your heart tell you that also?"

The officer's eyes flashed. "*Mon Dieu, vous êtes intolérable.* He has not *run away.*" The words were uttered with disgust. "It is more likely that he is lost on the moor."

"A man who knows every inch of the district? People who know the moor do not get lost except in a mist, and there was no mist last night."

"There are—oh, what is your English word for

'*marais*'? Places where you step in and you cannot get out."

"Bogs," the agent supplied laconically. "Dr. Leland would know better than that."

Memory stirred in Crissa, of the day when Paul had stood before her in the drawing-room at Grimstone, his boots caked with mud, his breeches stained. He had accounted for his dishevelled appearance by the fact that he had forced his horse too near a bog and been thrown. She turned to her companion.

"Mrs. Barlow, what this French gentleman says is perfectly true. Dr. Leland would not run away from whatever unpleasantness he believed he might have to face. Why, only yesterday afternoon as he left Grimstone, he said he must soon show his face in Tavistock or people would think he had broken his parole and vanished. Some misfortune must have befallen him, I am sure." She looked around at the group swelled now by curious passers-by. "We cannot just stand here and wait for him. We must try to find him."

"Where do you suppose the search begins?" the agent asked in a superior tone which infuriated Crissa. "The moor covers a somewhat large area, Miss Conway."

"Oh, do not be so obstructive!" she exclaimed in exasperation. "Someone must know where he went after visiting this farm. His housekeeper, perhaps? Or he may have told the people at the farm if he was going to another patient before coming home."

The woman who had spoken first put a hand on Crissa's arm. "Nobody knows where he went, m'dear.

We've asked, you see. So far as anyone knows, he was coming home from Magpie Farm."

"Then, surely, the obvious place to search is along the route he would take."

A big man, red of face and dressed in homespun breeches and an old-fashioned coat, stepped up to her.

"I rode that route this morning," he said in a deep, slow voice. "I went to Magpie to inquire if they'd seen a heifer I'd lost. There weren't no sign of the doctor nor his horse. And there are no bogs on that part of the moor."

Crissa looked at the ring of faces. Except for the agent, the expressions on every one of them showed sympathy and anxiety. But they were, she saw, as helpless as herself. There must be something she could do, some way in which she could help Paul. For she was certain now, with a cold fearful certainty, that he was in trouble. She glanced upwards. Beyond the houses and the shops and the bustle of the town lay the moor. Miles of desolate heathland populated by a few isolated farms, the only living things the wild creatures. Was Paul somewhere out there, alone and hurt?

She could not have said what made her turn. It was as if Paul himself was speaking to her, and no one else could hear. But when she turned she saw, instead of Paul, the "black witch." She felt again the chill shiver down her spine. Despite all that Paul had said about the old woman, there *was* something frightening about her.

The crone glanced furtively about her, then retreated a few steps, beckoning Crissa to follow her.

"I'll tell 'ee," she said in a high-pitched hoarse voice. "I'll tell 'ee where 'e be tu."

Crissa looked at Mrs. Barlow. The older woman said quietly, "It is quite possible. She roams the moor at all hours of day and night."

The dirty, crooked finger was still beckoning. Crissa went forward as if hypnotised, and it was without conscious thought that she made a cross of her first fingers inside her muff. When they were out of hearing of the little group, the old woman's voice became a whine.

"I've had little to eat for a week past, save a crust of bread and some stale cheese." She paused, her mouth working nervously. It was some moments before Crissa realised what was expected of her. Then hastily she unfastened her reticule and drew out some money. The crone darted forward and snatched at it with her claw-like fingers.

"He'm down a mine shaft."

Crissa caught her breath. "Do you mean that Dr. Leland has fallen down one?"

" 'Course I do. 'E bain't such a vule as to climb down one of they for the pleasure of it."

"But where? I do not know the moor."

"Up to the old Silver Dagger workings, off the Okehampton road."

"When did this happen?"

The old woman tucked the money beneath her black skirts. "That I don't know. But if he'm not got out soon, 'twill be too late."

"If you knew this," Crissa demanded, "why did you not tell someone before?"

"Who'd believe me? They'm all afeared. I scared 'ee, didn't I, up on the moor?"

"Yes. But I'm not afraid of you now." It was, Crissa found to her surprise, a fact. When she begged for money, the "black witch" had become merely a destitute old woman deserving, as Paul had said, of pity rather than ostracism.

"Are you telling me the truth?" Crissa demanded, gripping the bony arm.

The black eyes looked straight into hers. "He'm down the Silver Dagger mine. You'll find un there. And then you'll know 'tis no idle boast that I've second sight."

"You mean, you have not actually *seen* Dr. Leland?"

"Not with these," the old woman touched her eyes. "But here." She tapped her head. "That maid of yours understands. She knows what I can do. So do they all, that's why they'm afeared of me. But not him, not the doctor. He'm a gude man, I'd not harm him. You'd best go at once if you'm wanting to find un alive."

Crissa turned back to the waiting group and told them what had passed.

" 'Tis true she knows a deal more than most folks," one of the women said. "But what would Dr. Leland be doing at the Silver Dagger? That mine's been out of action for years . . ."

"And nigh a quarter of a mile off his track," the farmer added. "No man in his senses would willingly go near those particular shafts. You'd best forget that tale, miss, 'tisn't likely in the least."

"Then what do *you* suggest?" Crissa demanded. "Since no one else has yet come forward with any helpful idea."

Mrs. Barlow said, "I think Miss Conway is right.

At least this is our only clue and should be tried. Mr. Batten . . ."

The big farmer avoided her eyes and shifted from one foot to the other. "You'll not get anyone to go near them mines, ma'am. You'm not a foreigner here like this young lady. You'll have heard the tales about the Silver Dagger, and the evil spirits that haunt the place."

"That is absolute nonsense!" Mrs. Barlow exclaimed impatiently.

" 'Tisn't then, ma'am," another man argued. "More than one man has tried to go down that mine and met a violent death for his pains. Why, 'tis said a hand comes out of the wall and cuts the rope and anyone climbing down falls to his death, and the next morning the body's laid out on the heather. 'Tis another of the old witch's evil doings trying to get us to go there."

Crissa hesitated, looking from the troubled faces of the little group to the old woman, fast disappearing along the street. The crone had known that Hetty was with child, without being told. She had known where the escaped French prisoner was.

Crissa thrust up her chin. "How far away is this place?"

"Matter of two to three miles."

"Then if someone will be kind enough to show me the way, I will go and search for Dr. Leland. I am not afraid of evil spirits or hands that come out of thin air. My fear is that while we stay here arguing and doubting, he may be beyond our help."

"Bravo, mademoiselle." One of the French officers stepped to her side. "If Mr. Creber will give permission, I shall be glad to accompany you."

"I shall certainly give no permission," the prisoners' agent said coldly. "It is simply inviting you to escape. Perhaps that was Dr. Leland's plan. I would not put it past him."

The young Frenchman's hand went to his left hip. But there was no sword there. His face coloured, then went white. His companion caught him by the arm and drew him aside. In that moment, seeing the look on the agent's face, remembering his expression of hatred as he looked at Paul on the night of the prisoners' entertainment, Crissa understood.

"He has cause," Paul had said. "It is a long story." And she had heard that story not an hour since, she was sure, when Mrs. Barlow had told her how Paul had delayed and been too late to save a woman's life. "The husband never forgave Paul," she had said. Mr. Creber was that husband, taking his revenge in every possible way.

Crissa turned away sick at heart. Paul might be dying at this moment, and it seemed as though all her efforts to save him would be brought to nought.

One of the women spoke, her voice shaking with scorn. "Be you gwain to let a young lady and a Frenchman put you to shame, James? If you don't go as she asks, there'll be no supper on the table for you this night."

The farmer hesitated, reddening, then he said grudgingly, "All right, missus. So long as Samuel comes along o' me. We'll need a stout rope. And mebbe . . ." He thrust out his unshaven chin belligerently. "Mebbe parson'd come along, just in case the 'Knockers' be about."

"What are they?" Crissa asked.

The farmer's tone was truculent. "The creatures you can hear knocking at the bottom of the mine when you know nobody's there. They'm wicked for sure, as you'd know, miss, if you'd lived on the moor."

"For shame!" his wife exclaimed again. " 'Tis nought but an old wives' tale, only 'tis the men as tell it. Now get along with you and fetch the horse."

They set out twenty minutes later. The farmer rode his broad-backed cob, with his wife on the pillion. Samuel, who had gathered implements and stout ropes, was astride a Dartmoor pony, and Crissa, although she was no horsewoman, was mounted on a quiet mare from the livery stables.

Mrs. Barlow said doubtfully, "I am not sure I ought to allow you to go."

"I am sorry, ma'am," Crissa retorted. "But this is one time when, if you do try to stop me, I *shall* defy you. I cannot just wait idly here while Paul . . ."

Her friend pressed Crissa's hand. "I understand, my dear. If there should be any trouble with your father, I will take the responsibility." She turned to the farmer's wife. "Look after Miss Conway."

"That I will, Mrs. Barlow," the stout woman answered cheerfully. "She'll come to no harm along of us. Now get on, James. And Samuel, take the young lady's rein. She's not used to horses, you can see that."

Some of the French officers insisted on accompanying them as far as they were allowed. Fervently Crissa hoped that her father was not in the garden of Grimstone House where he might catch a glimpse of the odd little party as they passed below.

At the milestone the Frenchmen halted. The Captain of Hussars who had presented Crissa with the carved schooner came to her side, out of breath from keeping up with the horses.

"We can come no further. The agent is a hard man. But we will go with you in our thoughts and pray for Dr. Leland." He smiled up at her. "*Le bon Dieu* will see that you are in time, mademoiselle. We will wait here to welcome you both back."

She held out her hand. "Thank you. You are very kind."

The farmer, urged on by his wife, set a faster pace and it took all of Crissa's concentration to stay in the saddle. She wished she were more suitably dressed, for a light gown and cloak, besides being out of keeping, proved uncomfortable and impeding.

They left the turnpike road and turned right on to a rough track and climbed steadily upward. At the top of a ridge the farmer drew rein and pointed.

"That's Magpie Farm. And over there is what's left of the Silver Dagger workings. Do you see any reason, miss, why Dr. Leland should have gone there?"

With dismay Crissa looked at the desolate strech of moor. The heather was thin and straggly, not a flower showing amongst the pale seed-heads. There was no bright yellow of gorse, and the bracken looked crushed and sodden. There was not a sheep or pony in sight, only a lone buzzard wheeling silently overhead. The deserted mine workings reminded Crissa of the tinners' shelter by the river, with the same jumble of stones and rotting wood and thatch. But here the sense of abandonment was emphasised by the emptiness and silence of the moor. The wind blew bitter on the ridge, straight off the northern slopes.

Crissa shivered and drew her cloak about her. Despite the presence of the two men, and the cheerful face of the farmer's wife, her spirits sank and she felt a terrible sense of hopelessness.

She said reluctantly, "It does seem unlikely that he would go to that deserted-looking place. But the old woman . . ."

"You shouldn't have listened to her," the farmer said, and Crissa heard the relief in his voice. "I reckon we'm wasting our time looking for the doctor here."

She suggested, not very convincingly, "Now that we have come so far, do you not think . . . ?"

Her words were lost in a shout from Samuel. "Over there, look. Beyond the gully. A saddle horse. The doctor's, surely?"

They all looked where he pointed. Between the tumbled buildings, Crissa caught a glimpse of the animal. It threw up its head and whinnied; then emerged from the old workings and trotted towards them, its reins trailing.

Samuel rode forward. "Come on, boy, then. Come on. Where's your master, then?"

The horse stood quietly while he examined it. "He's not injured," he reported. "It don't look as if the horse pitched his master down a mine. So if he *is* down one, how'd he get there?"

Crissa said urgently, "At least we know now that he must be near here somewhere. Oh, do let us ride on quickly."

They rode in single file down the old path to

the mines. She could sense the doubt in the minds of the two men, and with the reasoning part of her mind she shared it. But instinct drove her on, a blind certainty that Paul, as the old crone had said, was down one of the shafts which she could see more clearly now amongst the derelict huts. She could not guess, any more than her companions, why he should have come to this place. But come he had, she was sure.

The farmer drew rein again. "Better go ahead on foot now, 'tis too dangerous for the horses with the shafts hidden by bracken and such."

Crissa turned to Samuel. "Pray help me down."

"You can't go trapesing around there, m'dear," the farmer's wife warned. "Leave it to the men, now."

"I must go," Crissa insisted. "I will be careful."

Reluctantly the men dismounted and moved forward, Crissa following. They had gone no further than a few yards when, from behind a low wall, came a weird, unearthly moan. The two men halted, staring at each other. The sound was repeated, more loudly this time.

"What was that?" Crissa asked in a whisper. "Surely—it wasn't human?"

Samuel shook his head. His face was pale, his eyes big with fear. "No, that it wasn't. Let's get away from this place. No good ever came to anybody here. Even when the mine was working, 'twas a place of ill omen. More men were killed here than . . ."

Crissa, quickly recovering herself, exclaimed impatiently, "Oh, do not be so foolish. It is broad daylight and nothing could possibly . . ."

She broke off, catching her breath, as the sound came again.

Samuel was about to turn and run when the farmer slapped his thigh. "Well, I'm danged. Proper fools we be. 'Tis only my lost heifer. Look, there she lies."

Crissa, her heart beating hard, peered over the wall. The animal lay on its side, its eyes dulled, moaning dismally.

"That's why Dr. Leland came here!" Crissa exclaimed with sudden intuition. "He heard this creature in pain and came to help her. It was just what he *would* do. And in the dusk—for it must have been getting dark by the time he left the farm—he missed his footing." Desperately she looked around her. "Let us all shout together. Wherever he is, he may be able to hear us."

The men hesitated, still looking doubtful. Then they followed her lead and sent a great bellow echoing across the deserted mine. Crissa rised her hand and listened, straining to catch the slightest sound. There was something, very faint, immediately drowned by the moaning of the heifer.

"Oh, do be quiet!" she cried in exasperation. "Listen. Surely, from over there . . ."

She hitched up her cloak and ran forward. Samuel made a grab at her. "Don't 'ee rush like that, miss. 'Tis terrible chancy here with all they holes not filled in. Take it easy, now."

Impatiently she tried to free herself, but he kept firm hold of her. In another moment she realised how right he was for, hidden by a clump of heather just where she was about to tread was the entrance to a shaft. As fast as they could they made their way across the debris of the old workings, to where she believed she had heard a human voice. On this side the shafts were more numerous and she halted, at a loss.

"Let us all shout again," she urged.

When the sound died away she listened anxiously. Unmistakeably there came an answer, faint but not far away. It came again, and this time she located it, a little to her right. She flung off Samuel's restraining hand and ran forward.

"Paul. Paul," she cried, flinging herself on her knees beside one of the bigger shafts.

Peering down, she could see very little. The sides of the shaft had fallen away in places. The iron ladder was broken and hanging at an angle. A stone, dislodged by her weight, pattered down.

Paul's voice, sounding very weak, reached her. "Help me . . ."

"Are you hurt?" she called down.

"No. But I—I can't hold on much longer."

The men stood beside her, incredulity on their faces. "He'm alive?" the farmer asked.

"Yes," Crissa said thankfully. "But hurry. Oh, please hurry. He sounds so desperate."

They unslung the ropes and peered over the edge. "Can't see un. Where be you, Doctor?"

His voice came faintly. "On a ledge. I—daren't move. I can hear you but I—can't see you. Who is up there? I thought I heard—a woman's voice."

Crissa leaned perilously over the edge. "Yes, it's me, Crissa."

"Crissa? *Crissa!*"

The amazement and joy in his voice almost unnerved her. She forced herself to be calm. "Hold on, Paul. It won't be long now. I'll keep talking to you while the men . . ."

"They must be careful. It's so—dangerous."

The farmer was taking off his coat. "Reckon I'm the stronger."

"You'm also heavier," Samuel objected, tying a rope around his waist. "I'll stand a better chance than you. You'd best use your strength to pull us up, when I've got a rope around un."

Crissa was near to tears. Only a few minutes ago these men had been ready to turn tail, unmanned by the moaning of a sick heifer. Now they were vieing with each other to face real danger.

The farmer belayed the rope around a boulder and braced his feet against another. Cautiously Samuel lowered himself over the edge.

"Keep your fingers crossed they old Knockers bain't around," he said and grinned at Crissa. "Though I reckon if they had been, Doctor'd be stretched out cold on the heather by now. All right, James, pay out the rope."

As he started down, Crissa heard Paul cry out. "What is it?" she asked.

"A stone—hit me."

There was a sound of earth trickling down the sides of the shaft, pieces of rock plummeting into the depths. Crissa could hear Samuel's laboured breathing, and the farmer's grunts as he took the weight.

"Paul," she called. "Paul, are you all right?"

He did not answer for a few moments. Then he said jerkily, "The wall is breaking away. I can't . . ."

"Hold on," she urged. "Oh, darling, hold on. Samuel must be nearly down to you."

She felt herself falling forward, and forced herself back on to her heels. Closing her eyes, she prayed as she had never prayed before.

Samuel's voice came up from the darkness. "I've reached un. But I can't get a rope around him, there's no room."

"What do 'ee want me to do?" the farmer shouted back.

"Make my rope fast while I see. I've got a hold on the doctor but 'tis proper chancy. Have you get me fast, James?"

"Yes. You'm safe enough."

Crissa and the farmer waited while faintly the two men's voices sounded from below. The veins stood out at the big man's temples, his face was beaded with sweat.

"We thought they wouldn't last the night," he said reflectively; then, seeing her puzzled look, went on to explain. "Our William and little Bess. I mean, the time they had the diptheria. Terrible it was to see them and Mother and me so helpless. But Dr. Leland saved them both. And now . . ." He looked down at his hands, brown and calloused, gripping the slack second rope.

"And now," Crissa said quietly, "you will save him."

He glanced at her, and thrust back his massive shoulders. "Yes, miss, I reckon so."

He had scarcely finished speaking when Samuel shouted up, "Pull on the second rope, James. But easy now, I've only got it around his arm." After a moment he called again. "That's enough. He'm free now. I'll get the rope around his waist." There was another wait which seemed to Crissa endless. Then, triumphantly, Samuel's voice came up to them. "Right now, James. Pull."

A few minutes later Paul lay on the heather, face down, gasping for breath, his fingers spasmodically clutching at the dry stalks.

Crissa withstood the temptation to go on her knees and hold him close. Instead she asked, "Is there a brandy flask in your saddle-bag?"

He nodded, unable to speak. She began to run towards the horses; then, remembering the danger, went more cautiously. She heard the farmer's shout of triumph as he hauled Samuel over the edge to safety.

His wife was standing beside the horses, her hands covering her face. Crissa put an arm around her shoulders. "It's all right."

"I just couldn't look, m'dear. I just couldn't. You'm the brave one. They'm all safe? My James . . . ?"

"He was wonderful." Suddenly Crissa found herself laughing, a strange sound in this place. "Perhaps now they won't believe those silly tales about the Knockers and hands that come out of the wall and cut ropes. No one cut those ropes."

The laughter dissolved into tears and her hands were trembling so much that she had difficulty in unbuckling the straps of the saddle-bag. But she found the flask and went back with it as fast as she dared.

Paul was sitting up now, his back against a boulder. The farmer was flexing his arms, Samuel dabbing his cheek where a stone had grazed it. Crissa knelt beside Paul, and unscrewed the flask. He gulped down some brandy, then offered it to the two men.

He turned to Crissa. Despite his ordeal he was smiling and his tone was almost gay.

"I might have guessed *you* would lead the rescue party."

"I told you, if you were in danger, I would find a way. But I did not think it would be—like this."

The farmer's wife joined them, picking her way carefully over the debris. "You'm a lucky man, for sure, Dr. Leland. If 'twasn't for this young lady you'd not be sitting there, looking as if you've come back from the dead. My man and Samuel may have hauled you up, but 'twas Miss Conway as found you." She cast an appraising glance from Paul to Crissa, then beamed at them both. "Ah, I see how 'tis, then. Come along, James, 'tis high time you saw to your heifer."

"The heifer can wait, Mother," her husband said, coiling the rope. "We can't just leave Dr...."

"Oh, yes, you can," she insisted. "And you can come along too, Samuel."

"But, missus . . ." he began to protest.

"Oh, come along, do," she urged, propelling both men before her. "Can't 'ee see when you'm not wanted?"

Crissa, the colour mounting to her cheeks, turned to Paul. "Are you sure you are not hurt?"

"Only bruised. Though how I escaped breaking my neck I'll never know."

"How long were you there?"

"I don't know. It was dusk when I heard the heifer and came across, and now . . ." He glanced up enquiringly towards the sun.

"It is nearly noon," she told him. "Oh, Paul, it

must have been dreadful, and I—I didn't know. All that time, and I didn't know."

"How *did* you find me?" he asked, easing his back against the boulder.

"The old woman—Phoebe's witch. She called to me and told me where you were." Then she was pouring it all out in jumbled sentences. "And it happened just as everything had turned out so well. You are not to be arrested and Hetty is to keep her baby, and Papa has quite forgiven her, and Aunt Clara spoke up for me. And then, you see, I thought it was all too late," she ended in confusion.

"Too late for what?"

"I thought I'd lost you before I'd even . . . before you'd . . ." She broke off, covering her face with her hands.

For a few moments he did not speak. She could hear the lowing of the heifer and the men's voices raised in argument. Then Paul drew a deep breath. He sat forward and took her hands from her face.

"Look at me, Crissa," he said gently. When she did so, he asked, "Before I had even told you that I loved you? Is that it?"

She caught her breath. "Are you—telling me that now?"

"Of course. I've been such a fool, fighting my love for you, thinking it a weakness instead of the strength it really is. And I thought it was Armand you'd given your heart to—until yesterday. Even then, I wasn't free to tell you."

"Because of that silly threat of arrest? As if that need have made any difference." She was suddenly very conscious of her position. She made to rise. "I think it is time . . ."

He still held her hands. "Oh, no, Miss Clarissa Conway. As you have told me on more than one occasion, there are times when propriety and decorum should be ignored. This is one of them. Crissa ..." He pulled her towards him.

She glanced over her shoulder. "Not here, Paul, not with ..."

"Crissa, stop arguing. When a man's just been brought back from the dead, he's in no mood to wait for an answer. Will you marry me, Crissa?"

"Yes," she said at once. "Yes, of course. And I haven't the least intention of arguing with you, any more."

Then she was in his arms and the little group on the far side of the old mine workings were forgotten, and Armand too, and Hetty. This time she knew, she had truly given her heart.

# Regency Romances
## by
# Elizabeth Renier

| | | |
|---|---|---|
| 27985 | The Generous Vine | 75c |
| 34410 | House of Granite | 75c |
| 36335 | If This Be Love | 75c |
| 67695 | Prelude to Love | 75c |
| 77755 | The Spanish Doll | 75c |
| 80730 | Tomorrow Comes the Sun | 75c |
| 85925 | Valley of Nightingales | 75c |

*Available wherever paperbacks are sold or use this coupon.*